THE LOWLY PROPHET

THE LOWLY PROPHET

A STORY OF HEALING, TRANSFORMATION AND AWAKENING TO LIVE AS A CHRIST

MARK HATTAS

POWERED BY THOUGHT LEADERS PRESS

PRAISE FOR THE LOWLY PROPHET

The Lowly Prophet is a heartfelt and thought-provoking read. Its blend of mystical experiences and relatable human struggles makes it an excellent choice for readers interested in spirituality, mental health, or personal growth."

— Literary Titan

*"It's **more than a book. It's an experience.** ...something I needed ...could feel myself changing as I read it."*

— Robert Slayton, MSeD, CFO Strategist, and Author

*"The way you presented Jesus as a friend and confidant **changed the way I talk to Jesus.** I really love that."*

— Dawn Kristy, JD, Founder and former CEO of The Cyber Dawn

*"This is the **best self-help fiction novel I have ever read.**"*

— Dr. Loren Michaels Harris, CEO Trajectory TV

"*...much more than an engaging story. It's an inspiration, a compendium of life lessons, **a formula for improving life, and getting closer to God** and your Divinity.*

— Joseph Gabriel, Founder, Optimal Condo Solutions

"*I resonate so much with this because **Jesus is extremely fun in your book,** and he's always been fun for me.*"

— Charan Prabhakar, Actor and Producer

"*I **feel more aware,** like something opened me up and brought me into a bigger experience.*"

— Pierre DeBar, Culture & Performance, HAP Training

"*This is amazing. I actually read eight chapters last night. **Couldn't put it down.***

— Zach Penprase, Mindset Coach, Former Pro Baseball player and Olympian

"*It's a tangible, accessible **reminder that we can all live as Christ.***

— Celina Ruhala, Artistic Director, Ruhala Holistic Arts Center

"*This book sparked the perfect co-creation between God and my authentic self. It **showed me the path to trust and true freedom!***"

— Gina Johnson, CEO, GJ Trading Company

"I keep being surprised by joy as I read The Lowly Prophet *& find it unwinding old, even generational, tales about my mind, whether individual or collective. I am hopeful this book's message will develop resilience in families & society."*

— Vienna Dunham, Learner and Hope-Bringer

*"It **helped me see God** not as distant, but as a friend— someone who **is always there, ready to listen and guide**. This book is an inspiring reminder of His presence in our lives and is truly a **must-read**."*

— Elizabeth Hall, Founder & CEO, eezenaturalhealth.com

*"The Lowly Prophet **reminded me of what's possible when we are truly aligned with God**—Jack's journey sparked self-reflection and a release of thoughts and emotions blocking my ability to fully listen & respond to Divine Inner Guidance.".*

— Denise Coelho, Teacher and Coach

*The concept of breathing in the Spirit of God into every place of my body... **that changed my life**, and the clients I've shared with. It has this peaceful, 'total alignment' effect. **Grateful to have found this book!***

— Michelle McClain

"The most compelling aspect of the book is its honest portrayal of mental health and spirituality... It's a testament to the book's power that it doesn't shy away from the messiness of life while still offering hope... The Lowly Prophet lingers long after the last page is turned."

— Literary Titan

"This book is a profound gift to humanity. *Poignant, timely & pivotal. Incredibly supportive & transformative. With my whole heart, Thank you!"*

— Angie M. Bruce, MA, Harmonizing Wholeness, LLC.

"Loved The Lowly Prophet! It opened my heart to a level where deep healing has occurred. **Felt enveloped by unconditional love and left with a deep abiding peace after the read.**"

— Phil Dugas, Breathwork Detox facilitator

CONTENTS

FOREWORD

By Stefan Andreas Junaeus
Editor-in-Chief, Thought Leaders Press

Every once in a while, a book comes along that doesn't just speak to your heart—it transforms it. When Mark Hattas first brought me the manuscript for *The Lowly Prophet*, I anticipated an intriguing read, but I had no idea I was about to embark on a profound journey that would awaken something deep within me.

As someone who has dedicated my life to helping others craft messages of purpose, influence, and transformation, I recognize genuine authenticity when I see it. Mark Hattas has delivered not just a story, but a living, breathing testament to the potential hidden within every human struggle, spiritual awakening, and seemingly ordinary moment of life.

Jack's journey in *The Lowly Prophet* is raw, deeply moving, and refreshingly real. I've walked alongside Jack through his struggles and victories, witnessed intimate moments of divine encounter, and observed with awe as he discovers what it truly means to "live as Christ." Mark's courageous exploration of mental health, prophetic spirituality, and the transformative power of inner healing isn't merely inspirational; it's revolutionary.

At Thought Leaders Press, our mission is to amplify voices that shift perspectives, elevate consciousness, and unlock human potential. *The Lowly Prophet* achieves exactly that—and much more. This is a book that will leave you profoundly changed—not because it teaches something entirely new, but because it awakens truths you've always deeply known yet perhaps have forgotten: that your life is sacred, your journey matters, and your awakening can ignite significant transformation in the world around you.

I'm honored to have played a role in bringing this remarkable book to life, and I'm genuinely excited for you, the reader, to embark on your journey through its pages. Prepare your heart, open your mind, and expect transformation.

Stefan Andreas Junaeus
Editor-in-Chief, Thought Leaders Press
Author of *Your Breakthrough Year*

GUIDING THOUGHTS

We are called to live in God as a Christ just as a caterpillar is called to live as a butterfly. Like all before you who awakened to this, there is a journey to take. This book activates that journey. Are you ready?

The people of this world are amazing and beautiful at their core. Yet, the false images we construct to meet our needs distort our true selves, leading to inner conflicts mirrored back to us through our realities. I, too, fell into this trap without realizing it, until a profound transformation awakened me to a deeper truth.

This transformation inspired the pages that follow. I am excited to share The Lowly Prophet, where Jesus extends to you a grand invitation through stories, characters, and divine mysteries unfolding in Jack's life as he learns to live as Christ.

"Christ has no body now but yours."

ST. TERESA OF AVILA (Widely attributed)

BEFORE YOU BEGIN
Enhance Your Journey

Reading *The Lowly Prophet* will spark transformation within you. This book stands on its own as a powerful guide, yet if you feel called to deepen your experience, you can take it even further.

How? By engaging with **The Lowly Prophet Transformation Journey**, an interactive companion program with lessons, immersive exercises, and community support.

Why? This digital program, used with the story, is one of the easiest ways to embody Jesus' teachings from *The Sermon on the Mount*— bringing the Beatitudes to life as daily practices for transformation. These are the same practices that led to my full restoration after a mental health crisis in 2011, and they help countless others deepen their faith and live as Jesus called us to live, as another Christ.

Go beyond the pages of the book and **apply its powerful lessons in real time**. Throughout *The Lowly Prophet*, you'll find **NEXT STEP** sections with **QR codes** inviting you to walk the path Jesus laid before us.

Already Signed Up?	**Not Signed Up, but Want to Learn More?**
Scan to access *The Lowly Prophet Transformation Journey* and begin with the "Welcome!!!" lessons	Scan to explore how this journey can support your transformation.

thelowlyprophet.com/tlp-nextstep	thelowlyprophet.com/tlp-journey

Your journey starts now.

CHAPTER 1
THE CRASH

My nephew turned seven years old the day Jesus physically arrived in my life. Though I had spoken to him constantly, this was the first time I actually saw him.

Amidst the celebration and surrounded by family and friends, I distinctly recall holding a piece of vanilla cake on a red, white, and gold paper plate, a superhero barely visible beneath the sugary delight. Before taking a bite, I glanced up amidst the chaos of moving bodies and saw a familiar figure standing beside the birthday boy. Between me and the open sliding glass door, which led to quite a lush backyard paradise, was Jesus. At least, I thought it was him. Tall, shoulder length brown hair, and neatly trimmed beard, this man appeared to be right out of central casting. Donning blue jeans and a long sleeve crew neck, he blended in, but his eyes. His crazy, beautiful eyes seemed to transport me to another dimension and my life-matrix glitched. His appearance changed instantly. His hair was longer. A white tunic tied with a red and brown embroidered belt replaced his modern look. Just outside, beyond his bare feet, were wooden sandals adorned with sturdy leather straps.

Once I re-established eye contact, he motioned for me to follow. This man, who appeared to be Jesus, headed outside, strapped on his sandals, and walked away. Stunned, my jaw literally dropped.

"You look like you've seen a ghost," my sister shared casually as she squeezed by me to the kitchen sink carrying frosting-filled utensils.

I was at a loss for words, only getting out "I, uh…," before abandoning my attempt to respond. Moving toward the door I wondered if I would find this mysterious man, or if it had been some type of hallucination. I crossed the threshold holding my breath. Looking past the familiar faces gathered in small groups, eating, and chatting away, I was drawn to the naturally formed grotto resting 100 yards back. It looked like a sanctuary, surrounded by colorful plants and vines, anchored by an expansive oak tree. Flowers covered the ground and an angel stood tall off to the side of a stone bench. The angel was also made of stone, but the man sitting on the bench looked very real. I made my way toward him, and as I arrived, he patted the bench with a smile, encouraging me to sit.

"Can I tell you a story, Jack?" the man asked.

"Who are you?" I quipped back.

"Who do you think I am?"

"Jesus?" I asked, realizing just how ridiculous that sounded coming out from my mouth.

"The one and only."

"How? Why? I mean, really?"

"Yes, really."

Despite wanting to doubt it, I knew it was him. I could feel it. It was like that time in junior high school when I spotted my friend Johnny at Disney World from three rides away. No one believed me, but I knew it. It turned out to be true, and we got to spend that day together.

I then turned away from Jesus for a moment as my mind started spinning, trying to figure out the situation. An unsettling feeling came over me as the echoes of insecurities crept in. He noticed this shift and said, "Jack, you are afraid of being tricked. I assure you this is no trick. Let me show you. You will find me to be a lamp for your feet, a light on your path" (Psalms 119:105).

He reached for my hand, and I let him take it. His touch instantly transported me to the famous sermon on the mount where I witnessed Jesus speaking to the multitudes. Despite his Aramaic tongue, I understood his words. "And that, my friends, is your way Home to the promised land God has prepared for you. Celebrate and be glad for all the prophets before you have gone on this path. You are all invited. Use this practice and it will lead to purpose, happiness, and fulfillment. You will restore to the wholeness God (Abwoon in Aramaic) intended for you. Now, we have work to do." Then, amidst the thousands gathered, Jesus looked right at me. I blinked and found myself back in the grove with... Jesus. My doubts subsided. I believed him.

"Jesus, what just happened? How did you do that? You are him; I mean, you. It's really you!" I smiled from ear to ear. My hero, my childhood hero was in my midst. Holy cow!

As if waking a child from a dream, Jesus repeated my name gently to get my attention, "Jack. Jack. Jack."

I needed a moment as euphoria mixed with my processing our short trip to ancient Israel. "Yes. Yes, I'm here. I'm listening. What do we do? What's next?" I was so excited, like a kid in a candy shop after years of deprivation. He laid his strong, weathered hand on my right shoulder. A rich warmth flowed through my arm, calming me down. I took a few long breaths and shook my body until the soft din of the party returned to my awareness.

Suddenly there was a strange, rather loud interruption. The voice of a desperate man broke our silence.

"My ambulance crashed. Oh my gosh! My leg. My leg! Help! I'll bleed to death. Jesus, heal this in the name of the Father and of the Son and of the Holy Spirit. Amen."

As I looked at Jesus on the bench, it was still just the two of us, despite hearing this frantic third man speak as if he were right next to us. Jesus's lips hadn't moved. It was perplexing.

"What did you say?" I asked Jesus, curious if he heard it too.

"Oh, nothing to be concerned about. We have been interrupted by a prayer from a friend."

"Oh, I get it. You're 'on the job', right?" I asked, curious how he would answer.

"No, that's not how it works. I'm not Grand Central Station or a busy phone switch from the 1930s. I am in tune with my friends, though, and a friend is calling out for help."

"Do you need to go?" I asked.

"No. Christ is taking care of it."

"What do you mean? Aren't you Christ?"

"Yes, but… Jack, come sit down for this one." Even though he had invited me to sit, I stood in awe. "I'm always Christ, but Christ is more than you've understood so far in life." Jesus smiled, patted the seat next to him again and asked if I wanted to see what he meant.

I did. I sat, and this time, he touched my arm. Suddenly, I was outside my body, looking at the two of us on the bench. Then, I felt a nudge and began floating away with the sensation that I was flying. The pace quickened until everything around me blurred. And then we stopped. A demolished ambulance appeared before me. It had been struck head-on, as evidenced by its crumpled front end. The offending black Mercedes was in disarray, blocking the otherwise quiet intersection.

Though the ambulance driver was unconscious, nearby a nurse and paramedic coughed and regained their balance.

The night air hung heavy from a recent rain. Streetlights illuminated the slick road as smoke from the crash rose above us. A man of dark complexion was visible through the ambulance window holding his right leg, rocking back and forth, writhing in pain.

Being there felt surreal. Despite knowing my body still physically sat on that bench in the garden, I very much perceived that I was at the crash site. More senses started activating as I caught words coming into focus as if my hearing in this alternate dimension was being tuned, "Consider it a gift," Jesus spoke to the soul of his injured friend. As the man bled profusely, his wife opened the ambulance door and rushed to his side. She created a tourniquet and quickly stopped the bleeding.

"How did you know I was here, Marie?" The man asked.

"I didn't. Jesus came to me and said I was to help him save one of God's children. I saw an image of an intersection and rushed here as soon as possible. Just as I arrived, I heard you yell, 'I'm in here. Help me,' and I knew exactly what I had to do."

"But how did you know how to create a tourniquet like that?" He asked, wincing, and knowing she only had experiences with the simplest of first aid: Band-Aids, gauze, antiseptic, and the like.

"I didn't know," she replied. "My hands just did it. They created the tourniquet like they'd done it a thousand times." Tears rolled down her face. "I could have lost you, Marcus. I am so sorry you were in this accident. How are you feeling?"

He stared down at his hands and said, "honey, I had a dream that I saved God from a massive heart attack and woke up panicking. I thought I was dying and called 911. I ended up in this ambulance, and... we crashed. I'm such a mess. I keep messing things up. You would've been better off finding someone more stable. I'm scared. I caused this crash. I'm at fault. I'm sorry, Marie."

CHAPTER 2
AN UNLIKELY FRIEND

"Don't be silly. You didn't cause this crash. It was a train wreck from the beginning. We need to get you some real help. That leg needs more treatment right now." She looked around for anything that might assist.

Then Jesus told me, "Jack, go touch his leg and heal it."

"I wouldn't know how," I replied. Besides, it looked disgusting. I was never much of a blood person. Anyone seeing my cringing face at that moment would have known. Jesus must have known it too, for he commanded me, just as a parent might to stop a child from running into the street, "Let go of the idea that you need to know how and trust it is possible. Allow your heart to open, and God will do the work. Touch his leg."

Instantly, energy flowed from my heart like a rushing river through my now luminescent arms and hands. My *body* moved toward Jesus's friend, and I touched the wounded leg. Energy poured out from me and into him.

"Owww," he yelped, reacting to my touch.

His wife, still searching for supplies, spun around, deeply concerned. "What is it, Marcus?" They were the only two visible life forms in the back of that ambulance. Neither had touched the leg, yet Marcus felt something. Was it me? Was it God? I didn't know. It was all new to me.

"Something is burning in my leg. Ouch. Oh, gosh. Make it stop!" Marcus grimaced as he held his breath and, through tears, he locked eyes with Marie, saying, "This is intense! Something's happening in my leg. It feels like someone's hands are in there moving stuff around." He breathed through the pain and then looked down in shock. The bleeding had stopped. The pain was gone. His wound had healed.

"How is this possible?" She asked as he slowly untied the tourniquet.

"The only thing I can think of is that I prayed to be healed just before your arrival. Perhaps God is showing mercy on me. Perhaps Jesus answered my prayer. It's a miracle." He laughed and jumped off the gurney, hugging Marie and bouncing on his legs. "It's a bona fide miracle!"

By that time, another ambulance had arrived. They attended to the wounded and were just about to open the door when Marcus burst out joyfully with his wife.

"You're, ok?" The newly arrived paramedic asked in disbelief. Everyone else involved with the accident was incapacitated.

"This is impossible. How did you survive this without a scratch?"

"I healed God," Marcus replied.

"You what?" The paramedic asked.

"I healed God by telling him what to do."

"I don't understand," the paramedic said.

Confused, I said to Jesus, "I thought *I* healed him."

"Through your actions, you did. You allowed the healing power of God to move through you." Jesus spoke, but my eyes stayed fixed on Marcus.

"Then why is he talking nonsense about healing God?"

"It's not nonsense. It is true," Jesus replied.

"How so?" I asked.

Jesus turned to me. *Oh, my gosh, is he beautiful ... Wow!* His body was made of light with all the shapes, curves, and lines of a physical body. I could tell it was him, but wow, he embodied perfect love. "Let me explain," he started, "Marcus has been diagnosed with a severe mental health issue. He has a notion that he is God in the flesh. He also thinks that makes him superhuman. As a result, his mind reconciles the fact that he prayed and is now healed. Therefore, he healed God. Make sense?"

"Well, if you step inside his delusion, it makes some sense. But in our world, that's insane. He'll be locked up if he keeps that up." I had some experience with the mental health system and had a sense of what was about to happen. "Jesus, he's not going home, is he?"

"No," Jesus replied flatly. "He will be taken to a behavioral health facility for evaluation. He'll be ok, though. He's going to have a massive healing in that facility."

"How do you know?" I asked.

"Because he will become a leader in this world, and that can't happen in this transition state. He has to heal, and you're going to help if you're willing."

"Yeah, right. How will I know how to help a man heal from a

major mental illness? I know nothing about that. I wouldn't know where to begin."

"Yes, you do. You're here with me, aren't you? I will tell you exactly how to help him." Jesus looked as confident as I did in my sixth-grade spelling bee when I knew how to spell *phenomenon* but hadn't started spelling it yet. I remember smiling at my mom as the judges and audience silently waited. She could see that I knew. I could see what she saw in me that day in his eyes.

I still wanted more, though. "And how am I going to get to him? I'm not a doctor, and ... oh, no. No, no, no, no. You want me to go there as a patient, don't you? No. Please, Jesus. Please."

I had been in a mental health facility multiple times, diagnosed with bipolar disorder, anxiety, and depression. I didn't want to go back. It would just show how much of a failure I was. I wanted to be healthy. But Jesus wouldn't say something to me that wasn't going to happen, would he? No, he was preparing me with this pre-cognitive gift.

Traveling faster than lightspeed, I suddenly returned to my body back in the grotto. Lying face up, staring up at the oak tree, I heard Laura say, "Are you okay, Jack?" She stood over me, assessing the situation, and continued, "I think it's time we go. Thomas has a game tonight." Our son played baseball for his high school.

"I don't know, honey. I might stay home."

She knew something was up, as I never missed a game. "Jack, are you ok?" She pressed.

"Yeah, yeah, I'm fine. I'm fine." I got up and looked for Jesus, but he was gone from the bench. Acting as normal as possible, I walked with Laura toward the house.

"What were you doing out here?"

"Ummm, praying. Yeah, talking to Jesus. Let's go." And we did. During the entire car ride home, I was silent as I wondered what I should share with her, and she wondered what I was doing at the grotto.

LATER THAT NIGHT

Everything went black, and time ceased. At least it had for me.

I woke to lights in my eyes and a sharp antiseptic aroma mixed with a hint of latex. A man in medical scrubs reached over me to turn off an alarm.

"How are you doing, Jack?"

Apparently, I had been unresponsive.

"Jack. Jack! There you go."

My eyes opened wider, and I recognized the face.

"You'll be ok, Jack. We had to give you a little something to calm you down. What is the last thing you remember?"

"I remember climbing out the window. I fell and then woke up here," I replied groggily.

"Do you remember what you were wearing, Jack?"

"Nothing."

"Right. Do you remember why you were climbing out the window naked?"

"Yeesss," I replied slowly.

"Can you tell me?" It was Dr. Specter, my psychiatrist, asking the questions. He was at my bedside in the ER.

"You wouldn't understand, Doc." I was awake enough to know that anything I said would absolutely be used against me—at least, that was my perception. The doctor tried to do his job and help as he knew how.

"Try me. I want to help," he said.

In a moment of weakness, I shared the truth. "After our son's game tonight, I felt dizzy and went to bed early. I woke up immersed in the sound of a loud heartbeat. The room looked rather strange, and I had this feeling that I was about to be born. Some dream, I guessed. Anyway, I was so excited and wanted to run free as God made me. I wanted to show the world my new body. I felt so alive. That's why I went out the window, to live."

"You know, I can relate to wanting to run free, but there are laws of nature that we all must abide by, Jack. Gravity is one of them. Next time, can you go out the front door? At least then, you would only be breaking an ordinance and not putting your life at risk."

"Ok. I'll remember that," I replied. What I failed to tell Dr. Specter is that my bedroom had transformed into an actual womb. It felt soft, warm, and dark. My only birth-day exit was through an opening, which was our bedroom window. I figured if I told him that part, they would lock me up and not let me go home.

In the end, he didn't even need to hear that part, because he admitted me to the facility anyway. Technically, I *volunteered,* but didn't feel I had much of a choice as he said he would admit me involuntarily if I refused. They soon wheeled me out of ER and over to my version of the 'looney bin'.

It took me a day to accept where I was. They weren't going to let me out unless I complied with their rules, including taking whatever pills were put in front of me. Ugh.

My second day began with what I thought would be breakfast. Everyone on our floor gathered at the front desk to sign out for the cafeteria. A counselor unlocked the main door and led us through a maze of corridors and down some stairs to join a line of people. Soon enough, I had my tray of taco salad with a side of chips and salsa—my first clue it was lunch, not breakfast.

The eating area was surrounded by windows, with several large round tables seating eight to ten people each, and rectangular two and four-tops filled the space. The music of Kenny G quietly played in the background. There was a lot of chatter, but I just wanted to be alone and found a quiet table in the corner.

Halfway through eating, a familiar looking man asked to sit with me. He introduced himself as Marcus. It was Marcus from the ambulance! He wore red sweatpants and a light gray hoody with the words "God lives" in small print across the chest. He had the build of an athlete who hadn't kept up his physique. Football was my guess.

Wasting no time, I asked, "why are you in here?" I could already guess the answer.

He looked down at his tray filled with pepperoni pizza, chocolate chip cookies, and a soda. "I had a panic attack," he began in a discouraged tone. "As I was rushed to the hospital, our ambulance got in a wreck." His eyes drifted, looking off into space. "It was so amazing, and I'm having trouble reconciling what happened. I could have sworn my leg had a huge hole in it, gushing blood. But, by the time the paramedics arrived, there wasn't a scratch on me. My wife can't corroborate my story, but I swear she was there. She tied the tourniquet around my leg." With a smile, for the first time his eyes turned to mine and tears welled as he paused. "Then I felt this burning, and... Well, the wound healed almost immediately. It was a miracle. I am so confused. The doc tells me my brain made the whole thing up, that it was all in my head."

"Why is that?" I asked, incredulous that the man wouldn't be believed.

"Because my wife died three years ago so she couldn't have been there. I feel so angry. I've been having these hallucinations since her death, and I want them to stop. I want to be normal. I'm scared that will never happen. I'm really scared and, oh my gosh, I miss my wife."

I felt so much compassion for him, knowing what it's like not to be believed. Little in life was more frustrating for me than being dismissed as crazy. Without thinking, I blurted out, "I was there, Marcus, at your accident."

He looked surprised, naturally, then confused as he rattled around in his memories. "No. I would remember you. Why would you say something like that?"

Despite him clearly feeling irritated, I continued. "It's true. I saw your wife tie a tourniquet around your leg. Jesus was there." I told Marcus the whole story, but he still had trouble believing it. I knew the facts, but he wondered how that was possible. Marcus turned his head away, his eyes fixed on empty space as he gently bit the inside of his cheek. Finally, he looked back at me and squinted.

Then I said something that surprised myself. "Jesus is going to speak with you tonight. He'll tell you. Watch and see." I knew Jesus would speak to him that night just as I knew the sun would rise in the morning. I knew because God spoke with me, and I learned to listen. My soul had healed so much since the days when I had blocked God's love and therefore all the insights that were there for me to receive. God's messages were on a very different *frequency* in me and were always supportive. In that sense, I *knew,* or trusted, at least, that Jesus would speak with him that night.

God had been retraining me for some time before Jesus showed up at the party. Even early on, messages came through occasionally. One time, the message was so visceral as God appeared to be alive in everything. The Holy Spirit came over me at that moment and seemed to strip away all that kept me from a relationship with God, everything that kept me sick.

Like many who have *God* moments, I thought I was done with my issues for good. I thought I was done with *crazy,* but clearly, I had at least one more round of insanity to go. Despite God guiding me to heal, I still felt that I was failing. I wanted this time to be the last, and in a message received the night before, he promised me it would. I didn't know if that meant I'd die before being admitted again or that I'd heal. According to His word, I was ready to become a priest.

I was not so sure. After all, my version of a priest wore a collar and said Mass on Sundays. They did other things, too, but you get the idea. God told me I'd be a different type of priest, the type outside of traditional churches. He said I'd find out what that meant soon enough. It felt distant as I was in a hospital doing the hospital thing. I'd have to wait and see.

Marcus continued staring but shifted his glance up and down my body. My slim frame was no match for his heft if he indeed was sizing me up to fight. Appearing to conclude I wasn't worth it, he gave a dismissive huff, shaking his head in disbelief before leaving. To him, I was just another crazy person on his wing, where he perceived he didn't belong either. I wondered if I'd made a mistake telling him all that.

That night I got ready for bed and prayed to find the strength to do whatever God needed while in that hospital. Sleep came quickly.

THE MISSION

"Jack, wake up. Jack. Hey, it's me, Marcus." Marcus was two inches from my face, whispering so he wouldn't wake my room-mate. It was the middle of the night and I knew why Marcus was there. "Jack! It happened. Jesus came to me."

I sat up, told him to give me a minute, and I would meet him out in the lounge. After he left, I called out to Jesus and asked what I was supposed to do.

"Be present and let him tell you the story," Jesus said.

I went out to meet Marcus, who was glowing with giddy excitement. He couldn't wait to share Jesus's message, though my enthusiasm was tempered by how tired I felt. "Ok, Marcus, lay it on me."

"Jack, you won't believe this. I was dreaming, and Jesus

showed up in the dream. He told me that you healed me. You saw my wife in the ambulance. You saw the whole thing. You were there."

"Yes, I was."

"I believe you. Now, you must believe me. You are a prophet. God speaks to people through you. You must get healthy. You have one thing off in you that's blocking God: your denial of your prophetic nature. That is why you're here today. You had to see for yourself that God is using you for His plans."

I didn't expect his story to include me. Suddenly, I perked up and leaned in. "Go on."

Marcus continued. "You will meet a teacher next week. And this teacher will share everything you need to build a church in this world that has no boundaries. It has one purpose: to awaken people to God's love and restore life. You're going to change your perception of a lot of things beginning with yourself.

"Jesus showed me how you thought you were healed before. He tells me you can only get there fully with this teacher. Trust her when she arrives in your life. Thank you. I am not crazy. My wife, though she's passed on to the other side, has been coming to see me. She showed up with Jesus tonight. She had a message for me. And I'm letting go of her now. She wants me to move on. And I have you to thank."

"How so?" I asked.

"You sacrificed your freedom to save me. You didn't need to be hospitalized. There was another path, but Jesus had you come here because you want this barrier between you and God healed. You are a hero in my book."

"Dude, chill. The only hero in this story is God. Bless you, though." I shooed him away. "Please, go now."

"Why would I do that?" Marcus asked, unsure why I wasn't sharing his enthusiasm.

I held back the tears, hoping he would leave, but he stayed. "Honestly, Marcus, I'm afraid of being used by God. People project their darkest fears on his messengers. They always have. And I feel terrified. I'm willing, but I am feeling so scared. Do you know how crazy it sounds that you and I had our encounters, but how real they are to us? People won't understand. They can't understand until they have eyes to see and ears to hear. Something is happening to people; I think I know what it is.

"Perhaps I am a prophet—a humble, lowly one at that—hesitant to fully embrace the call. Yet, despite my reluctance, my life has been transforming. Changes are happening so quickly. I want to trust in Him even more, but the leaps of faith seem to be growing. I know Martin Luther King, Jr. had it right: I need to take the next step in faith even though I can't see the whole staircase. I'm still scared, though."

"You should be scared if you only focus on how people will react." Marcus said. "However, if you keep your eyes on God, you will become fearless. Jesus told me that, too. Jack, you'll be fine."

REFLECT & CONNECT
Chapters 1 & 2

Before moving forward, pause to reflect on your journey so far.

CH. 1: Encountering the Divine: In Chapter 1, Jack encounters Jesus as a friend and guide, challenging his understanding of spirituality. Have you ever experienced a moment that felt deeply spiritual or "otherworldly"? How did it impact you and your beliefs?

CH. 2: Recognizing Our "Unlikely Friends": In Chapter 2, Marcus becomes an unexpected guide for Jack, helping him accept his role. Have you ever had someone unexpectedly help you see a deeper truth about yourself, or have you spoken into the life of another this way? Care to share in the portal?

DIVE DEEPER - Join the conversation. Explore more thought-provoking questions and share your insights inside the **O Coalition Portal**.

Scan the QR Code to Enter the Discussion

thelowlyprophet.com/ tlp-reflect&connect

NEXT STEP
Walk the path. Live the transformation.

The Lowly Prophet Transformation Journey (TLP Journey) is your **guided path** to integrating the tools from *The Lowly Prophet* into your daily life. Through immersive lessons and practices, you'll **deepen your spiritual healing, mental clarity, and divine alignment**. Walk the path Jesus taught us, embrace the wisdom, and step fully into who you were created to be.

Scan to Apply TOOL 1 and Deepen Your Transformation

thelowlyprophet.com/tlp-nextstep

TOOL 1: Conscious breath

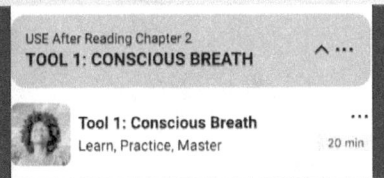

1. Go to the "Learning" tab and open the course
   (On top navigation menu in desktop, or bottom menu via phone)

2. Locate TOOL 1 in the Syllabus

3. Watch, Read, and Practice the exercises.

4. Use the exercises **WHILE** reading Chapters 3 & 4

Objective: Retrain your body's natural response to stressful situations, allowing yourself to remain calm, conscious, and focused even in the face of challenges.

CHAPTER 3
THE CHRIST

A few days later, I was released from the hospital. Jesus greeted me at the exit with a celebratory hello and warm embrace. His khakis, white polo, and Air Jordans fashioned a dorky dad trying to look cool. The only difference: He looked cool. The hair helped, as it looked a lot like Jonathan Roumie's from *The Chosen*. "I told you that you'd be just fine. See. All patched up. Are you ready to go?"

"Go where?" I asked, still getting my freedom legs under me as we walked across the parking lot. You would think I'd be ecstatic leaving the hospital, but honestly, I was still tired from the effects of heavy medications. With a duffle bag of dirty clothes over my right shoulder and Jesus at my left, I caught his eyes smiling in the glimmering sun as I awaited his response about our destination.

"To your teacher," He answered. He was funny. He had this way of laughing without laughing. He said stuff, and it was filled with all the unsaid things he knew about but had yet to reveal. I suppose he was at play, having fun with me, everyone. He was joyous, genuinely joyous.

"I thought you were my teacher," I replied.

"I am, but we need a human being for this next part. I found just the right woman. Join me, and we'll go far together. "

"Haha. Yeah. Let's go. I hope she has better food than the crap in there."

"Food? Where we're going, we don't need food." Jesus was playing on a quote from the movie *Back to the Future*. I wasn't sure if he was being funny or if some mystical training was to take place where food would no longer be necessary.

Shortly into the drive home, my divine passenger faded from sight, but not before telepathing an image of the teacher's address an hour's drive north. Oh, was it nice to be home, if only briefly. After a meal with Laura and our son, Thomas, a short nap and a quick shower, I left for class. As it turned out, it was a training course with real people in a real town and real food, all very... normal.

Well, she was a little peculiar, the teacher, but what can you expect from someone who has surrendered her life to God and now exhibits spiritual gifts that leave most in awe? As a child, I might have considered her magical—something I reserved for holy people, like saints and prophets. Before experiencing prophecy myself, I couldn't comprehend that it was possible in

21

modern times. In fact, I was quick to judge, assuming most who claimed such gifts were phonies or frauds. I may have been wrong. Even as it unfolded before me, it remained a mystery—profound and deeply moving.

PROPHETS

The class took place in a beautiful 1930s stone mansion surrounded by dozens of acres of pasture and woodland. Inside, walking down a few steps to a great room off the kitchen, plush carpet welcomed my sock-covered feet into further luxury. The natural lighting, high ceilings, and new construction smell led me to believe renovations had occurred recently. A couple of decorative couches and several wooden dining chairs framed the outside of the room, leaving space in the middle for floor seating. Cushions for further comfort were stacked near a white marble fireplace beyond a large whiteboard securely stationed at the front.

James, a courteous older gentleman, welcomed me to his home and said that Mary Jo, our teacher, would join shortly. He pointed to fresh snacks and beverages in the kitchen, all prepared for the ten or so participants expected. Having arrived early, he took the time to share how he'd met Mary Jo serendipitously at an auction and that his life hadn't been the same since. Upon my further inquiry about her, James said I would find out soon enough and excused himself to welcome another guest.

After grabbing a cushion and sitting for a few minutes with my eyes closed, I felt a tap on my shoulder. Jesus had arrived.

"So, what do you think?" He asked, sitting next to me and admiring the space. After scanning the room, he looked outside and shared, "early settlers blessed this land, which has been a sanctuary of celebration for over two hundred years. Before that, it was a home to wildlife, relatively untouched following the Ice Age. I've had four families occupy this space, all with hearts of gold and doing work to bring more people to God. So many memories are here. If James gives you a tour, ask to see the secret room under the stairwell. He'll know who told you." Jesus leaned back and pointed toward a large mirror in the foyer with a wink.

"I'll do that, but before Mary Jo arrives, can you tell me about her?" I asked, more interested in the class than secret rooms.

"Sure thing. You are going to like her. The best spiritual teachers have taught Mary Jo, who supports bringing wisdom from the ancients forward to the present day. Along the way, she discovered that prophets existed everywhere in history. This is where you come in and why you are here. Like you, she used to think prophets were *magical creatures* that only lived in Bible stories." He chuckled as he danced his fingers about whimsically with raised eyebrows. "The truth is that prophets, before they know themselves as prophets, traverse through the inner realm of their being, transforming while collapsing anything in the way of union with God. Like with you, Jack, a metaphorical space purifies within them becoming an anchor point for expanded purification until all is restored. Throughout this process, spiritual gifts are activated, prophecy being just one possibility. Imagine an apple seed finally resting in fertile soil with perfect conditions. That seed will naturally grow into a tree and yield fruit. It's the same with this. You may be early in the fruit bearing years, Jack, but trust, it's happening."

"I am trusting you. So far, though, Jesus, I continue to look crazy." Hearing that leave my mouth gave me pause. Still navigating the complexities of a mental health diagnosis, I was torn between the world's message that I would never be healthy and the divine one that I was transforming into something more than I had ever dreamed. The latter would be considered grandiose thinking by my psychologist.

Seeing the tension on my face, Jesus comforted me. "Jack,

relax. Imagine a tiny door inside your heart. The key to opening that door is dismantling all that is unlike God. This is accomplished by attuning to the active forces of God, which is the result of Rookha d'Koodsha, also known as the Holy Spirit. You are in good hands. Trust the process."

As my peace returned, his use of an Aramaic phrase, *Rookha d'Koodsha*, caught my attention. "Rookha d"koodsha?" I asked.

"Yes, Rookha d'Koodsha was a divine feminine word often translated as Holy Spirit. She breaks off the effects of your errors, anything unfit, and teaches the truth. She also instructs people on all matters related to their path *home*. This immeasurable force upon your mind is always in harmony with God's Laws and what is divinely intended for you. And, by the way, one result of trusting Rookha d'Koodsha is being tuned to receive communication from God. Of course, this is known even in psychology. Famous psychoanalyst Carl Jung described it as an all-pervasive web of interconnectedness between the Divine and the worldly." Jesus paused to let His words sink in.

"Wow. So Rookha d'Koodsha does that for me? And, once that door in my heart opens, my spiritual gifts activate?"

"She does it with you. Your free will gives you the choice to allow action in you to take place. If you do allow it, you will mature quickly, and your divine gifts will come alive. Opening that door is not the finish line but a step forward to your new life."

A woman standing nearby moved closer and spoke as if she had been part of our conversation all along. "And, Masters of these gifts," she shared, "including prophets, have one thing in common. Do you know what that is?" She questioned me.

"No," I replied.

She knelt before us and softly shared, "The purity they seek. Their off-target behaviors and thoughts, also known as sin, cut them off from the active forces of God. Therefore, true prophets are vigilant about purity. Just as it would be obvious that your alarm was going off in the morning after a restful sleep, sin to someone with a refined spiritual body is *alarming*. No constructive action can really be taken until that *alarm* is dealt with or the sin is forgiven and released. It doesn't mean these people are incapable of sin, but they detest it as the effects are immediate and undesirable." She paused, and Jesus stepped in.

"Jack, meet Mary Jo."

Mary Jo was an elegant woman in her sixties. Her high cheekbones and moderate proportions were complimented by a black high-neck midi dress and white slippers. Yes, white fuzzy slippers. Silver-streaked layered hair framed a smile that I'm sure melted many hearts, and a unique flower of life pendant graced her collar, highlighted by a gold cross.

"You must be Jack," she said, extending her handshake as we stood. "I see you're with my favorite Master Teacher. Do you know this?"

I nodded. She was the first person I knew of who could see Jesus with me. I suppose everyone else just assumed I was talking to myself.

"Then you also know," she continued, "that he brought friends." I did not know that. "He brought a lot of friends," she said as her eyes glanced to the ceiling and then around the room.

"Is that okay with you?" Jesus asked her.

"It will keep me sharp," she replied before turning her attention back to me. "If you are like me, Jack, you might have thought prophets came out of the womb ready to serve. That's just not how it works for most of us. We all went through what you are going through now but in our own way. There is a formation process that prepares the *soil* for the seeds of prophecy. The Bible shows this with the relationship of Elijah and his disciple, Elisha. We see the already-formed prophets of the Bible but not their formation. Formation is critical, regardless of a person's gifts and talents. Whether it's Jeshua's disciples, you, or me, we all have our formation paths. During those periods, developing prophets have experiences to train their systems and learn to trust their new abilities.

"New sensations, movements, desires, and ways of seeing, speaking, hearing, and knowing are refined along the way. Early on, you may hear an inner voice break through the clutter of mind *noise* with the resonant frequency of divine love. Over time, that can become the only voice heard in your mind. You will learn to trust *knowing* without knowing, *seeing* without seeing, and much more. I am so happy you are here."

"So, do all budding prophets question and doubt along the way?" I asked, exposing my current insecurities.

"Good question. All prophets are formed from unique starting places, and God accesses each person where they are, just as a good teacher educates a child in their preferred learning style. I'm reminded of my son, now in his thirties, with Central Auditory Processing Disorder. The first day of kindergarten he could only learn his address and phone number by singing it in a song. First, he could retain the melody, then the words. Just as his skills developed over time, yours will, too. You will be called into action and stretched into your new capabilities as they do. How does that sound?"

"The truth is, Mary Jo, I'm concerned about screwing this up. It somehow feels way more important to get right than anything leading up to this point," I replied.

"You'll fail from time to time. That is certain, but all your weaknesses and frailties are already known. Just as a child is trusted with clearing the table before progressing to washing dishes, you will be trusted in small things before larger ones appear. You'll be okay. As my teacher once told me, if you stay aligned, you will succeed. Any other questions before we get started?" she asked. Most of the group had arrived, but a few were still gathering refreshments.

"Yes, I suppose I do. You seem delightful, but I'm still wondering why Jesus doesn't teach me this himself."

As if sharing a mind with Jesus—for she phrased it like he would—she replied, "Jack, what you learn in this class will open a channel to heal deep-seated wounds that persist in your lineage. You have a block to becoming the prophet Jeshua knows you will become. It is a fear that no one will care, and you will be subjected to scorn in this lifetime. Jeshua brought you here because this is where you need to be."

I liked her and felt like I was in the right place.

"That said," Mary Jo continued, walking to the front of the room and lifting her voice so everyone could hear, "you have a message that needs to be shared. In fact, if you indeed share it, your message has the capacity to heal anything, anytime, anywhere. You have a message for the ages that will require you to change. If you do, your message will reach people, and rightfully so. You will open something in people, accelerating their relationship to Christ. A ten-year path to live as Christ could be collapsed into months with the right teacher and willing student, and that goes for all of you here today." The group had fully gathered by the time she paused.

"Yes, all of you will learn to awaken the teacher within a person, and they will have a chance to live a life beyond what they've known as one in being with the Divine. God is consciously accessible in your life right now, and accessing and sharing this is masterful. But you have no idea how, do you? So, you have come here. Let me teach you. Let me show you how to approach God's love with an open heart and let that heart be purified completely. Then you will know how and delight even more in the glory of what Jeshua calls Abwoon."

"Abwoon?" a woman nearby asked. I'm glad she did as I recalled hearing Jesus use that word before.

Mary Jo explained, "Abwoon is an Aramaic word translated to 'Our Father' in the Lord's Prayer. It means the great source of life that births forth all creation. Neither masculine nor feminine,

Abwoon reflects the life force, the substance, the God from which we come-our 'father.'"

Like a baby held and rocked to the rhythmic hum of a parent, I felt *held*, nurtured, and in good hands. Others appeared to feel the same way as I noticed smiles, relaxed faces, and affirming nods. My eyes landed on Jesus who pointed my attention upwards. A dozen people, all dressed in white, watched from a virtual loft above the room.

I asked him in a whisper, "Who are they? And by the way, would you prefer I call you Jeshua instead of Jesus?"

"They are in-betweeners," he said. "They have a block to loving God but have expressed interest in opening up to learn more about Him. They need to unlearn what they were taught in their lifetimes and learn what God actually is. That requires a teacher, and Mary Jo is exceptional. As for my name, in my native Aramaic tongue, it was Jeshua, but many call me Jesus, and I respond to both. The name doesn't matter nearly as much as the love behind it."

"Got it. Thanks for bringing me here. I feel happy. Thank you."

Mary Jo led the class in a breathing exercise and prayerful meditation to help us center and connect with God's Love within us. She announced we would clear out the mental trash cans cluttering our minds. "Ask the following question and wait for the answer," she guided us as we lay on the floor. "Don't *try* to answer. Release your inclination to figure out the 'right' answer and allow an answer to come. Here's the question: *What am I?"* She explained we would receive the answer we needed to support collapsing the lies we held and all we made up about ourselves.

I said, "I release figuring this out and allow the answer to come." Then, after a few breaths, I asked, "what am I?" and waited. Eyes closed; my breath nearly stopped in what is called a still-point breath. Then the answer hit with a rush of excitement. We all received answers and shared them with the group. They were all different.

During the exercise, I forgave the images I perceived others made up about me. I forgave and released the thoughts and images I perceived about myself. I landed on who I have always been, love, the love I was made in the image of. The words, "I have Christ in me, and I am seeking to know more and more of who God is" came through my lips as I shared with the group.

There were gasps from two people in the room. "That's blasphemy. How can you say such things? That is false," One of the two expressed with condemnation that Christ was in me. I felt a pressure build. I wanted to run. This was the scorn I feared (at least a flavor of it), and I felt distressed as the second woman supported her friend. "You may have Christ in your heart, but to say that He lives within you as if you've become Christ is not only theologically incorrect but borders on blasphemy."

My throat tightened, my hands started shaking, and I even felt a little dizzy.

People began murmuring, and Mary Jo let it flow.

"Jesus, why are they reacting like that?" I whispered under my breath.

"Like many people, they think Christ is an individual. But in my home, kings, priests, and prophets were anointed with oil for their divine mission. This symbolized their sacred calling and God's empowerment for the roles they were to fulfill. These were anointed ones—the messiahs. That term evolved to signify a future Jewish king anticipated to rule the Jewish people during the Messianic Age.

"I fulfilled the messianic prophecies of the Old Testament, and my life, death, and resurrection opened the way for all to step into this fulfillment—to live as Christ. As Jack the Christ.

Laura the Christ. Thomas the Christ. Every person who accepts this call becomes *Alter Christus*—another Christ—not in title, but in being. My body was never meant to be the last; it was the first of many. Every individual expression in Christ is a living fulfillment of God's promises, ushering in a new heaven and a new earth, a world transformed, consecrated, and restored from the fall. It's happening."

"It is?" I asked.

"Yes. That process of consecration begins in each person by activating Rookha d'Koodsha, The Great Unwinder of all errors and comforter to those who truly seek God. The moment you surrender into that truth, the undoing begins. You become whole in Christ. Sustaining that takes time." Jesus continued. "Much more on this later. For now, relax. Breathe. Watch. You will be just fine."

The murmuring quieted, and all eyes turned to Mary Jo who challenged me by asking me to explain.

Flustered by the attack and despite Jesus telling me what to say, I felt overwhelmed. "Mary Jo, I'm really feeling off right now, uncomfortable, and nervous. Can you give me a minute to settle down and process all this?"

"Absolutely. While Jack is doing that, if you believe he is wrong, I challenge you to allow your belief to soften. What if you have been wrong? What if the one who taught you was incorrect or at least incomplete in their understanding? Are you willing to allow information that conflicts with your point of view to be witnessed? Perhaps we can all learn something from one another."

I appreciated how Mary Jo calmed the group, giving me time to center. "Jesus," I said, "may God present to this group. I surrender to you, Lord, and trust you in everything." I took a breath and waited for the words to come.

Like sheet music, I *read* the words God placed in my heart. "In the beginning, there was only God. This invisible force of power and life birthed from the non-physical to the physical." I looked around, consciously making eye contact with each person before continuing. "Life in the physical emerged in automatic succession, evolving constantly.

"Human beings could eventually inhabit this planet. We had a lot in common with other life forms. But there was something different, apparently about us. We had the capacity for a conscious relationship with God. We did this collectively for some time, and then Jesus broke tradition and opened a direct relationship with God through what we know as the Christ. *Christ* was a descriptor for someone who cracked the code on God, shifting to a new life. It required dying to the world's ways and rebirthing into a new life. But to the observer, nothing changed physically.

"Those individuals who embodied Christ's teachings seemed unchanged in appearance, yet they were profoundly transformed within, aware of their newfound identity. For a moment, think about a caterpillar recognizing its massive changes as it emerges from its chrysalis, reborn as a butterfly." Rising from my seat, I approached the whiteboard.

Mary Jo graciously passed me her marker and stepped aside.

WHITEBOARD

After sketching a caterpillar, I elaborated. "Envision this caterpillar engaging in its daily routine until one day, it feels a compelling urge to create a simple silk pad. Firmly attached to a branch, it sheds its skin to reveal the chrysalis, its cocoon for transformation. It goes with the flow of what's happening, with no resistance. Perhaps it feels anxious. Perhaps it is a little unsure of what is happening. But it knows this is its life path. But what if the caterpillar resisted the silk emerging from its body? What if all the caterpillars living in our fictional *Caterpillar Land* judged the chrysalis process and shamed any caterpillars showing the first signs of creating their silk pad? Resisting this natural process would be difficult and lead to resentment, anger, and likely depression or other diagnosable illnesses. Wouldn't those caterpillars look insane fighting against this natural process? There would have to be an outlet for that pressure."

I took a moment to let that sink in, watching as people took notes. "As humans, we also have a natural process to change from one version of ourselves to a transformed and awakened one. This transformation story is everywhere. Star Wars' characters become Jedi Knights. Neo accepts his role as *The One*, aiming to free humanity from The Matrix. Simba becomes the Lion King restoring the pride lands. Harry Potter finds his place in the magical world. In the real world, we awaken as Christs. Though, after the change, we don't look noticeably different on the outside, we are radically different on the inside. It's the ultimate hero's journey.

"Like the caterpillar story, resisting this natural process leaves people feeling lost, dislocated, angry, frustrated, fearful, anxious, depressed, and even manic.

"If what I'm saying is true, then knowing this, wouldn't it be insane to resist transformation? People can keep up their resistance for many years or even a lifetime, but eventually it gets hard. Dissociations, distractions, abuses, and addictions hide our desires and keep the changes at bay. Yet even the strongest of us playing this internal tug-of-war will wear down and face the recurring decision to drop the rope or fight on.

"We can learn to consciously face our denial and resistance, invoke the Holy Spirit to activate a healing process, and allow the change just as every caterpillar allows its metamorphosis. You don't have to know how to live as Christ. But you must stop fighting it and learn what is optimal to heal your soul. You have an option to live as Christ.

"Jesus was the Christ, inviting us all to union with our Beloved Creator. This restorative process is for anyone who says yes to it. We are all invited to the *banquet*, but who will say yes? We are called to live as he lived, and who amongst us will heed the call? He shared the path to restoration at the Sermon on the Mount, but how many of us practice his methods? He taught the path so that we can have what he had, a fully restored relationship in union with God."

I paused and checked in internally. I frankly was in awe of the words coming out from my mouth, which didn't come from thinking as I had before, but a flow, like opening an audiobook and listening to its message. Looking at Jesus for guidance, He nodded and motioned for me to continue. I did.

"God will call each of us home. You will be led to Christ by the Holy Spirit with its active forces of God guiding you *home*. Jesus showed us in the Beatitudes how to activate a latent guidance system in each of us. When active, He shares the many promises that will come. I'm here to tell you that I have practiced these, and they work. The promises are real. Do what Jesus said, and you will change for the better and experience purpose, happiness, fulfillment, and well-being."

Jesus gave me a hand sign to pause there.

"Mary Jo, how are we doing?" I asked, exhilarated.

"What do you all think of this?" Mary Jo asked the group. "Would you like Jack to continue, or are there questions or comments from anyone?"

A young man sitting on the carpet raised his hand and said he would like to know what to expect as a Christ and what happens after the transformation process. Mary Jo invited me to answer.

"Well, the purification elevates our consciousness, alters our perceptions, and opens access to the Mind of God. This has been called infinite or creative intelligence, right-mindedness, and Holy thinking. This access opens even more over time as our willingness to change increases and our fears dissolve. As Jesus taught, we shift from being of this world to being in this world but of God. It's a different *game* that Christ *plays*. Those in that state operate from a place of love, valuing souls finding their way to Christ as well.

"In that Christ state, things that once held your interest no longer will, just as a toy no longer holds a child's interest as they mature. As a *newborn* Christ, you will learn rapidly. You will have all your memories, information gathered, and skills developed throughout your life, but in Christ, you will apply them in new ways. Just as there are developmental stages of a child, there are developmental stages in Christ. Having only known branches and leaves its whole life, imagine the awe a caterpillar experiences when it wakes up as a butterfly. The flight—the sights, the sensations, the new everything. It must be quite extraordinary, right? That is what it is like to wake up as a Christ. You experience awe again. You see with new *eyes,* a fresh lens on everything.

"You will experience fears losing their hold until eventually they have no say in your life. Christ lives as one connected with the whole and walks the earth as an individual who knows he or she is one with God. He will stand for what is just. She will take the right action, always from love, abiding as one with the active forces of God. The Christ receives Heaven on Earth.

"God wants this world purified. This is part of that purification. It will happen with or without you. The *prodigal son* chose to go home. You get to choose, too. We all do. Jesus gave us a map to get home no matter how lost we have become. Are you ready to use it? I've been using it, and the *map* is given to us by the Holy Spirit, and it always leads *home*.

"The day we choose to follow that map is a glorious day. That is the day we allow ourselves to be prepared for God's return. On that day, the end is near, the end of our off-target ways. If we choose to *stay* on that path, the end is certain, and so is the beginning, just as the end of a seed's life is certain when it is planted in fertile soil, and its life begins anew as a plant, flower, bush, or tree. Just as certain is your new life in Christ.

"Imagine that we can be restored fully in this lifetime! If enough of us do this, our world will soon reflect this restoration of individuals, families, communities, countries, and more. It's our choice. Jesus taught us how.

"I am a burgeoning Christ in this world. I invite you to live in Christ, too. Mary Jo, it may sound arrogant to some, but it is not. We can all say yes to God, and God will bring us all the way *home*."

"What do you mean?" One of the participants asked. "I agree with some of your messages, but please say more about God bringing us home. What does that mean?"

"I'll do my best. Imagine if God were a broadcasting station, and anything tuned to God becomes a conduit through which God is alive. The life force in a flower comes from this life force we call God, and it takes the form of a plant. Likewise, God *broadcasts* or expresses through each of us.

"What if we turn off our *antenna* or it is bent, broken, or tuned to something other than what God is? We would pick up whatever signal it's tuned to. As it turns out, we have a built-in repair shop (the Holy Spirit) that aligns our *antenna* to pick up the signal God is broadcasting through all of creation, and when the signal is pure, it will transform us until our consciousness is lifted to a pure state, the state of Jesus.

"At that point, we're in surrender and will be refashioned

into the image God created us in, the image of His Love. And then, we will function in the world as a living Christ, bringing about the good and the holy and the amazing gifts God bestows on us to help others find their way. In this *home,* we are one as God designed us, and the separation we once *knew*, or perceived, will have dissolved. There is no greater feeling. Yet, as human beings, we are still in the world. The difference is the world holds no power over us, as we have chosen freedom in the most real sense possible."

"I'm not saying I agree with you, "one of the initial objectors started, "but in your version of things, aren't you a victim to God in that you have no say over your life, that you have given up the freedom to do whatever God wants?"

"That's the fallacy," Mary Jo jumped in. "I'll let Jack answer in a moment, but I want to share that his insights are also on target with my teachings. However, there is an alteration I would like to make. In Jack's example, you have a separate relationship and are restored as if you were apart, which is impossible. You can never be separate from God, except in perception, as you are God in the truth of God. I'm not talking about the fantasy of a God who lauds over us and controls our lives, but the actuality of what is real in the most real sense.

"Jack is talking about God as the life force that sustains everything. Nothing exists apart from this presence. It is woven into everything that lives. And when all material things fade, what remains? God—the essence beyond all form. Our words, our stories, and our attempts to understand God will pass away, yet God continues to know and express through every living thing—like a flower. The flower might not understand complex things like Newtonian Physics, but it knows everything it needs to know to be the best flower it can be. It experiences life through itself.

"Likewise, God is known through the life of a single human who opens to this presence—who accepts or rejects it. When a human rejects their own essence, they reject God. But when they turn away from false images and illusions, they make room for God to express fully through them. Yet, the one who has severed their sense of connection with God, even if only in perception, may not know the way back alone.

"However, suppose that person chooses to heal and reconnect from this cutoff state. In that case, there is a built-in design to support the shedding of any obstacle to us living in the Christ body, and that is where God remembers itself through that one person and once again expresses, fully delighting in being a Mary Jo, a Timothy, a Karen, a Sam, or whatever name has been given. In summary, the issue is the perception of God as distant from us, as being somewhere 'out there,'" Mary Jo pointed up. "This Life-Force of God, is closer than your breath. It's right here, right now. However, we may have errors in realizing the truth as Jeshua knew when he said, 'My Father and I are one.'"

She closed there and we took ten minutes to meet each other, get more coffee, and stretch our legs. Stepping outside to a massive pavers brick patio, I noticed a picturesque pond through the trees.

Soon enough, Mary Jo reconvened everybody for the next exercise. After a brief meditation, she directed us, "now, ask this question and wait for the answer: *How do I remember what is true?*"

I sat in contemplation: *How do I remember what is true?*

What if God lived in all things? Wouldn't that mean every-thing is made of God? Wouldn't it all be God? The story in the Bible of us being all parts of one body then makes a ton of sense. I may be the 'finger' and be a great finger, but I am also part of the whole. I am all of it, even if my particular experience in life is as a 'finger'. If this is true, we owe it to ourselves to learn to live as one. Perhaps that's where this planet is headed.

"Why don't you help us live as Christ?" Mary Jo interrupted my thoughts, crouching beside me.

I'm not a teacher, and I have no idea how to help people do that. And then the words came out from my mouth. "Fine, I'll do it." *Ugh! What am I thinking?*

"Great, then it's settled," Mary Jo exclaimed. "Once you have finished answering the question you will see lunch is ready. Enjoy the next hour eating, enjoying each other, and exploring the property. After lunch, Jack will teach us how to become one in Christ."

Well, it's not that simple. Is it? I thought.

CHAPTER 4
SATAN'S GIFT

I laid down my pen as Jesus suggested going for a walk, which sounded perfect. James asked if I would like to eat.

"No, thank you, James, but could I see your secret room under the stairway?" I asked, grinning.

"Ah, so you're the one. I was sure you'd be taller. I'll meet you there in just a few minutes," he replied.

Everything about his response was odd. *I'm the one? Taller?*

After helping people settle with lunch, he found me near the mirror and opened it. The mirror, along with its frame, opened like a door, revealing a second made of thin metal that slowly lowered into the floor. He turned on a switch, which illuminated a stairwell leading downwards. "There you go, Jack. Enjoy," he said.

"You're not coming with me?" I asked, uncertain what I would find down there.

"Oh no, it's not for me. This visit is for you," James answered.

I took a step down and turned around to ask, "what do you mean, I'm the one?"

"Jesus told me he was sending a friend and that you might ask to see the secret room."

Realizing he also had a direct relationship with Jesus, the pieces clicked together. "So you knew everything I was sharing in there?" I asked.

"No, not exactly. Each of us experiences things uniquely. It was such a nice sharing. And, I suppose you were also learning as the words left your mouth?" He looked at me with knowing eyes.

He was right. Through Christ, I often felt an inner teacher speaking through me. As I taught others, I found myself learning alongside them. I nodded and began to make my way downstairs.

The floor from the foyer was made of thick reinforced stained glass and the sunlight caused an image of Jesus's mother, Mary, to appear below, just ten feet from the final step. Her light revealed a small octagonal church with ten pews surrounding a stone alter held up by boulders. It clearly hadn't been used in a while as dust covered every surface.

"What is this place?" I asked.

"This used to be used weekly, believe it or not," Jesus replied. "Many of my friends traveled here from the south, and even though this was a free state, it was far from welcoming to many of my brothers and sisters. State laws required residents to return freedom seekers to their owners. It was dangerous for people who had been enslaved to gather in groups. This was a safe house. Check it out."

Jesus pointed toward a dimly lit, downward-sloping path that opened to an old kitchen and then to some bathrooms and bedrooms.

"A hundred people could live down here!" I exclaimed, using my phone light to see better.

"It was more like fifty comfortably, but yes, it was a sanctuary unknown to anyone except for you, James, and perhaps a dozen others."

"Why are you showing me this?" A rag doll, a few clothing items, and a towel in one of the baths were just a few remnants of lives affected by this place.

"Because, Jack, you talk about Christ like it is a celebration, an achievement that is awarded at the end. It is a mission. You are joining a mission, and you will be asked to do what is right and needed, much like the family who created this. It was a wealthy family with a lot to lose. But they did what you are doing and our Father in Heaven, Abwoon, called them into action. They faced fears, were challenged, and acted anyway. As God transforms the Earth, many things need to change. You and everyone up in that room today are being called to help. God works through people. He worked through me, and though God is more accessible today because of my willingness, there is still much to be done. People died here, Jack. They had babies here. They celebrated birthdays here."

A wave of emotions created tears. Somehow, celebrating in the dank underpinnings of a mansion just feet above their heads felt so wrong.

Jesus interrupted my sadness. "These were joyous times, Jack. These fine people were on the road to true freedom. Despite this physical darkness, their inner lights were shining.

Today, their ancestors are creating memories of their own up where the light shines. This planet has people up in that sunshine living in darkness, and it's time to share the good news and free them, too. And as big as that opportunity may feel, you are not alone. Come. I want to show you more."

We walked further down a hallway that went quite a distance while fewer lights and narrower walls created a feeling of claustrophobia. "Is this the right way, Jesus?" I asked after five or six minutes.

"Yes, we are almost there. Reach up with your hands and grab the rope. Walk to the end."

Soon, I reached an arched wooden door secured with a rusty metal latch. With some effort, it creaked open, revealing a tall, cylindrical chamber lined with a hand-crafted ladder just wide enough for me to climb. The air was thick with darkness, and as I neared the top, I knocked my head on something above. I felt along the surfaces around me until my hand met a hollow sound —a false wall. With a gentle push, it fell away, revealing a dusty space beyond. Fresh grass clippings clung to the back tires of a large riding mower, and the presence of modern tools hinted that the shed was still in use.

As we stepped outside, Jesus and I found ourselves beside the backyard pond at least three hundred yards from the house.

"Hey, Jack, you know what my favorite memory was from my lifetime, my absolute favorite?" Jesus asked as we reached a nature path that wrapped around the pond. Tall grasses and wildflowers hugged the well-worn path.

"Turning water into wine?" I asked, knowing it was one of my favorite stories from the Bible. It was Jesus's first public miracle in a series of extraordinary events.

"Yeah, I figured you would say that, but no, that wasn't it. That was a good one, but not my favorite." He stopped talking, and I continued to walk.

"Well?" I asked. "Are you going to tell me?"

"I'm being with it. I can almost taste the air I was breathing at the time. I can feel the nerves push through my body upon hearing the voice say, 'Throw yourself down on those rocks. If God is who you say he is, he'll save you.' What a day!"

"That is your favorite memory?"

"Yes, it's my favorite."

"Why? Why would the temptation from Satan be your favorite? It would have been my most awful."

"Nah, I don't think so," Jesus continued. "It would have been your favorite, too."

"Why? What are you trying to tell me?" I finally let go of my perception and shifted to curiosity.

"God let Satan tempt me. It was the end of my forty days in the desert, and the story leaves out a critical element."

"Yeah, just what I need, another reason to have the Bible purists tell me I'm full of shit. 'Did you know?' I can picture myself saying, 'That your Bible is missing a critical element of the story of Jesus.' That will endear them to this message."

"Jack, you worry too much. This isn't for them. If it were, I would share it with them. This is for you right now. So, listen up."

"Ok, ok, I'm all ears." We sat on a bench just off the trail, and I focused all my attention on Jesus. "Go ahead, I'm listening." Despite our playful banter, Jesus was a wise master and a great friend. I loved Him with all my heart. He was so patient and taught only when I was ready.

He began, "I had generations of stuff to work through before beginning my ministry. Everything that could tempt me had a history. Everything that could pull me away from God had to be cleansed. I had a very bad situation that needed to be purified to step forth as the Christ and teach with authority."

"But I thought you were perfect," I stated.

Yeah, well... you're really stuck on that, aren't you? I'll share a secret. The perfection is in me as Christ. I was as human as you and had to do what you did. If I didn't, how could I have taught you so well? I did what no one before me had ever done. I got so clear on who I was that I rose after being crucified, another good memory. Nothing separated me and God, and I knew I'd come back. After I rose, I taught the Disciples at an accelerated pace. Most of them didn't understand my messages until that time. That is why I needed to do it, to help them wake up and spread this extraordinary message.

"Now, back to my favorite memory. Satan did me a favor and showed me where the last vestiges of fear lay within me."

Huh? I thought, having imagined him fearless all along. "You were afraid too?" I asked.

"Of course. You don't think I was a little nervous when Peter cut off that soldier's ear? But God had integrated so much within me that a tinge of fear was calmed with the trust of God's thought, 'Pick up his ear and heal him.' I had seen enough as a personality to know that voice and trust it in all things.

"Well before that moment, Satan appeared in the mountains. At that time, I was still relatively new and had not yet started my public ministry. Despite this, I welcomed the temptation, as I knew it was necessary for me to be at my best, and Satan is exceptional at revealing our weaknesses.

"The moment between his mockery and my response is missing from the Bible. You see, faith develops. It is tested and matures over time. Though well after Satan's temptation, I invited Peter to come to me on the water during a wonderful storm. Had he kept his eyes on me, he would have continued walking on that water. His faith was still developing. It's a process. My faith, by the time Satan tempted me on that day, had been tested, purified, and strengthened.

"During those temptations, I focused on God and breathed as sensations moved through my body, and thoughts from the generations flooded my mind. But soon, they all passed, a calm washed over me, and I spoke, 'Get out of here, Satan', or something like that."

"I think what you said, referencing scripture, was, 'Again, it is written, you shall not put the Lord your God to the test'."

"Yes, so I did, but I also killed him on that day."

"What do you mean?"

"I mean, I tore him limb from limb and killed him."

"You're kidding, right?" My mind showed an image of my peaceful friend forcefully ripping limbs from a little red, screaming, cloven foot, horned creature, and I was looking for Jesus to crack a smile.

"What are you feeling right now?" Jesus asked me.

"Discomfort. Fear. I imagine something quite disturbing and out of character with the Jesus I know, which is very different from the account I've read. Please tell me you are making this up."

"But it's Satan. Didn't he deserve it?" Jesus asked.

"I'm confused. Why are you doing this?"

He looked so serious. His playfulness gone. "Doing what?"

"Making me feel scared. Being weird. Are you who you say you are?"

"I am."

"And who do you say you are?"

"I'm Jesus, the one who rose from death after crucifixion two thousand years ago. I am, I am."

"Then why do I feel this way?" I asked.

"Because your fear is alive, and you are focusing on the storm. Keep your eyes on me."

He was right. I had gone somewhere in my head, dredging up my past with all the fears that came with it. "Ok. Ok." I redirected my focus to Jesus and asked, "What do I do?"

With the utmost compassion and care he led me. "Breathe, as I did when Satan tempted me. Let the fear move through you and stay in it until that *storm* calms. Give no heed to the images my words resonate in your mind about tearing someone limb from limb. Let the images surface and move like passing clouds. And now, let your perception of what I said change. Let go of the image you made up and hold to about that circumstance."

I did as Jesus instructed. I breathed, felt, and let the images, sounds, and ideas pass through me. Within a moment, the tension in my head collapsed, and my shoulders dropped. I consciously released the thought that I knew what he meant about tearing limb from limb. "Ok, Jesus, I'm ready. Now what?"

"The truth is that Satan will always bring up your issues. I was being metaphorical in my language, and you imagined me hurting some poor dude you dressed up in your mind as Satan. I used the metaphor so you could see this: I defeated Satan by keeping my eyes on God alone. You must learn to do the same and heal just as you healed this issue."

"Healed?" I asked. "What do you mean by healed?"

"When an issue has an unresolved emotional charge, a person can easily be deceived. The greater the charge, the more distorted the perceptions for that person can become. An opportunity exists to access that stored energy and allow Christ to open it up and release the hold. As these stored emotions move out from the body, resonant thoughts, ideas, and distorted memories will leave with it. They will transform as we allow our perceptions to change. That is when God's love activates new awareness within us. This adjustment is what I taught in the first three Beatitudes, and the fourth was to repeat them again and again, to hunger for God's righteousness, the pure source of Love available to all of us. That is a big part of spiritual healing. It affects the mind, body, and emotions as well. It is critical to defeating Satan in our lives. So, what do you say? Are you ready to purify your soul?"

"Yes, I am. I want this. I really want this."

"Ok, then. Let's get back to Mary Jo. Lunch will be over soon."

REFLECT & CONNECT
Chapters 3 & 4

Before moving forward, pause to reflect on your journey so far.

CH. 3: Encountering Christ: In Chapter 3, Jack learns more about what it means to embody "the Christ." How does this concept resonate with you? Have you ever felt a calling or inner pull toward something beyond the "you" you are familiar with?

CH. 4: Transforming Adversity into Strength: Chapter 4 suggests that facing adversity can build inner resilience. How have you transformed challenges or adversity into personal strength? What advice would you give someone going through a similar struggle?

DIVE DEEPER - Join the conversation. Explore more thought-provoking questions and share your insights inside the **O Coalition Portal**.

Scan the QR Code to Enter the Discussion

thelowlyprophet.com/ tlp-reflect&connect

NEXT STEP
Walk the path. Live the transformation.

Continue **deepening your spiritual healing, mental clarity, and divine alignment**.

Scan to Apply TOOL 2 and Maximize Your Emotion-Body

thelowlyprophet.com/tlp-nextstep

TOOL 2: Emotion-Body – Feel, Regulate, Receive

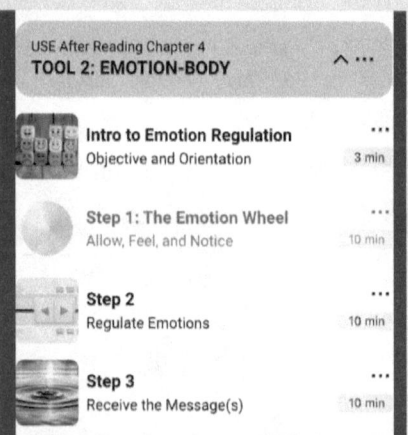

1. Locate TOOL 2 in the Syllabus

2. Watch, Read, and Practice the exercises.

3. Use the Practices **WHILE** reading Chapters 5 to 7

Objective: You will develop full awareness and connection with your emotional body. This means allowing emotions to arise and flow naturally, without resistance or judgment. You will practice experiencing emotions fully while remaining present, creating space for insights and deeper self-awareness.

The Emotion Wheel
(Use as referenced in TOOL 2)

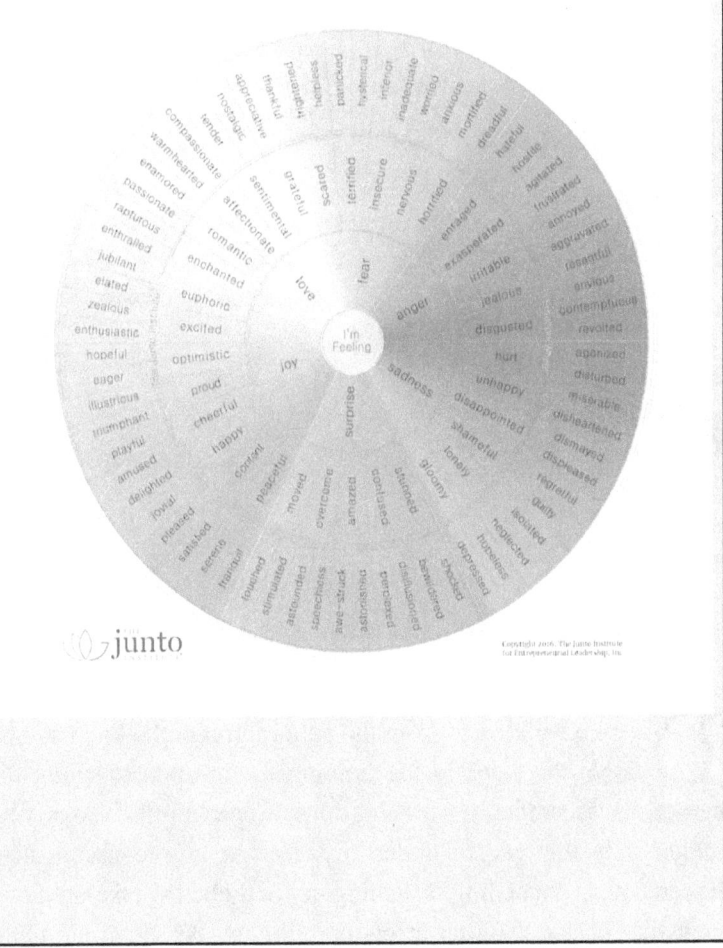

CHAPTER 5
WHO'S WHO

Despite walking in from the patio, through the kitchen, and down the steps to the training room, upon touching the carpet, I was suddenly watching myself entering the room. I no longer felt the carpet under my feet as my consciousness hovered near the ceiling, watching my body below take note of a new sign on the wall: an arrow pointing up. As the group gathered, Mary Jo returned, and a message appeared on the sign: It's now or never. I watched from above as *Jack* cowered from it, and I could sense his physical anxiety—yet I was detached from it.

"Jesus, are you there?" Jack asked. Silence. "Jesus? Jesus?" Nothing. Jesus was gone, or so it seemed. I continued to observe.

Mary Jo took the front of the room and began teaching. "OK, everybody. I have a list I want you to review. It is a lifelong effort to make a list like this. It has every issue you have ever had to deal with as a human being. It is a short list. There is only one thing on it. Can anyone guess what it is?"

Everyone looked around at each other, wondering who might have the answer. No one appeared to have a clue.

Jack whispered, "Jesus, where are you?" He felt naked and afraid. He was alone—he had never been alone. Jesus had told him that he had been there since the day Jack was born, but not now, not here. Mary Jo was his teacher today, and Jesus seemed to have split. Scared, Jack let out an expletive a little too loud.

"Jack, is everything alright?" Mary Jo asked.

"Yes. I mean, no. No, I'm flipping out here. I don't like this." Jack was panicking.

Mary Jo went to his side. "Lie down, Jack," she said, and he did. She put her hand over his mouth and told him to breathe through his nose. He was disoriented but listened. She touched his forehead and wrist, closed her eyes, and relaxed into a deep, tranquil state. "Breathe, Jack. Relax." Suddenly, an energy flushed through him, and he was calm.

"What did you do?" He asked Mary Jo as he sat up.

"I asked God to heal you. I was shown your childhood memory that seeded your fear of abandonment. This Divine Love moved my hands where they needed to go and shot a love process through your system. I imagine you feel better, but we're not done. I am going to have you say these sentences. They are commands to your system to let go of this issue. Are you willing?"

"Sure. Yes. Thank you." By this point, he was extremely appreciative of Mary Jo.

"Ok, the first is 'come to me, Lord, in my time of need. I release the burdens, which I perceive I placed upon you, and allow this change'."

Jack repeated the words and noticed a lot of emotion move through him: sadness at first, then anger, followed by joy. By the end of it, he was smiling. The other students had formed a semi-circle around Mary Jo and Jack, engrossed in the encounter.

"OK, Jack. Second sentence: 'Lord, I cancel my goal to replace Jesus at the right hand of the Father'."

Jack felt embarrassed but followed Mary Jo's prompts. Again, a strong wave of emotion flowed through his body. Thirty seconds later, the energy shifted. The whole room felt it, and instantly, he smiled again.

After indicating with a nod that he was ready to continue, Mary Jo said, "last statement, Jack. 'Whatever good can come from my life, I so appreciate all of it'."

This was a little more challenging for Jack to say. Resistance surfaced, and Mary Jo suggested he sit with the emotion before saying anything. "Begin when you are ready, Jack."

A few moments later, he felt a tapping on his shoulder. It was Jesus. "You've got this, Jack. Just trust." And with that, Jack repeated the prompt, inhaled deeply through his nose, and exhaled as a low vibrational tone rose up through him.

"Ahh-oooooooooom." This continued for about forty seconds and had the effect of shaking loose the last remnants of a lifelong issue. Like a baby giving up a pacifier upon maturing into a toddler, Jack allowed God to take away whatever was there.

"Good. Good, Jack. Nicely done." Mary Jo stood among the group as people shared their heartfelt appreciation for the experience.

"That was amazing,"someone said.

"I've never seen anything like it," another added.

The comments flowed in hushed tones, reverent of the sweet, sweet presence of God in that place. After exchanging a few warm hugs, Mary Jo returned to the front where she sat and closed her eyes, prompting the room to join her in a brief meditation before continuing the lesson.

Well, that was interesting, I thought. It was like I had an out-of-body experience as two apparently separate people in the same body. I was me as Christ and me as Jack simultaneously but separately. A part of me seemed to need attention, while another looked on as a witness marveling at the situation. It was certainly unusual. Jesus was back. I was back.

"What was that?" I asked, looking over at Jesus.

"Within everyone," he began, "divisions, or parts, have personas, and each persona must be healed until no separate persona exists. This healing of the divisional identity is necessary to consistently be God's trusted servant. And that is what you want. You will become this if you stay on this path."

Talk of divisions in me hit a nerve, "But, people who are crazy have divisions. I want normal."

"Correction," Jesus said, leaning in closer, "you have divisions in you, and there are truer words to use besides *crazy*. Try this: '*Here and now I choose God, and anything unlike that must transform into the authentic me.*' The false you must leave to experience God as you wish, in perfect splendor. Most people on this planet are divided internally and hide through mechanisms that have worked for them until now. Their *drug* of choice is not as effective as before. So, they will find new ways to suppress their fears and distortions even deeper. Or, they will heal."

This was exciting. "Can you share more?" I asked, intrigued that our repressive *drugs* of choice were no longer working as effectively as they had.

Lifting his hands to illustrate, he patted his chest and said, "their wounds, and beliefs, everything off-target inside them must correct (hands now palms up in front of him) to withstand the changing frequencies on the planet (fingertips come together like a steeple)." It will become harder and harder to resist (hands tighten into fists). The *reluctant caterpillar*, the metaphor you referred to, can only fight for so long. Eventually, it will transform or die resisting its transformation (hands continued *dancing* with his words).

We're moving toward a time when the world will begin looking even more insane as people find more creative ways to resist God's love, to resist the natural process of becoming Christ. People will fight to the death to hold onto their perceptions, which unfortunately will happen if they resist their transformation. But there will be a day when that fight ends, and people of the world will be aware and use this process fervently for the survival of humanity. That will be a day to celebrate, for heaven will be available to all. This will be sustained. God will have a home here, and it will last forever. People will no longer *sleep* in their consciousness but live awake, alive, and in tune with Christ and God's glory.

"You will someday witness this from a unique vantage point, but today is also a glorious day. Today, you have learned how to collapse the stories you told yourself about who lives inside you. Are you ready to tell your other parts that it is time to integrate?"

"I guess so," I answered. "I think so. Do you think I am ready?"

"Yes," retorted Jesus.

"Ok, how do I get started?"

Just then, Mary Jo called my attention to the whiteboard. "Jack, would you tell me what this sentence means?"

It read, *You have within you millions of parts all ready to function in unison in alignment as Christ.*

"Um, yes," I laughed at the irony that this was exactly what

Jesus shared with me. "It is the collapsing of perceptions that keep us from living as the whole human we are."

"Yes," she replied. "So, with that, what is the one thing on your list containing every issue you have ever dealt with as a human being?"

"Denial," I knew the answer. It had to be denial.

"Yes. Now, are you ready to end denial?"

"Yes," I said emphatically.

She went on to show how to release issues of separation within us. One of my *worst* offenders was a *bully* in me that I buried deep under a *nice* persona. When this inner bully finally surfaced, it challenged me with, "come on, show me what you can do. You want some of this?"

Uh-oh. Am I ready for this?

CHAPTER 6
EXTRASENSORY

As a kid, I was nice because that was how I was portrayed. For example, after sharing with a sibling, helping my dad with a project or my mom bake cookies, they would say I was "nice." I even received the brotherhood award in school for being "nice." But *I* didn't believe I was nice.

I shared with others so Mom wouldn't be disappointed, and I helped Dad in hopes I would get an ice cream. Helping Mom bake landed me in cookie heaven. The truth was I manipulated my surroundings to have my needs met. Behaving *nicely* also reduced conflict. I hated conflict. Conflict brought emotional distress, which I did my best to avoid. This led to, you guessed it, inner conflicts.

A common inner question growing up: *Do I say what I think, or should I agree to get along?* I tended to agree. Of course, I was lying to myself to get along—I used denial like a drug to keep my inner conflicts hidden. Denial kept me safe and justified my actions. However, deep in the recesses of my mind, there was a log of all the times I denied the truth. I had become so good at denial I hadn't even noticed how far I got from the truth of any given situation. But one day I learned from the bully that lived inside my mind. He was furious that I was so devious. I *saw* him occasionally, that inner bully, and *he* was useful in navigating my way through minor issues with force.

I remember one time when a peer challenged me to fire an employee. I had made the mistake of agreeing with this challenger all along the way. The employee in question had made some mistakes, and I went along with my peer's venting. This diffused her energy, and I continued my workday. But she kept bringing it up and found more evidence of incompetence from the same employee. She could no longer see any good in this person. It had become cancerous.

The truth was this employee had a lot of good in them, and I saw it. I began pointing the good out to my peer, which fueled an unconscious battle of who could find the most *good* or *bad* in this person.

While this unfolded, I collected issues about the challenger. After all, no one is perfect. One night, when she attacked me for not firing the employee she saw zero value in retaining, I whipped out my mental arsenal. I unleashed a verbal, *Incredible Hulk* tirade on this woman who cried *uncle* three minutes in. She didn't know I had it in me, but there it was, my inner bully for an audience of one to see. The challenger was shocked and terrified. If we were in a verbal fistfight, I brought a samurai sword and sliced her legs off at the knees.

My bully, which the world rarely saw, lived deep within me, and I loved it when it came out to *play*. Once it was out, it was effective at ending the conflict, which was my goal. The streets may have had *blood,* but my stress had reduced dramatically.

People didn't realize the depth of denial required for that bully to attack with such ferocity that no one dared stand in my way. It had the effect of vindicating my behavior leading up to that point, too. I felt a sense of ease, believing I had *taken care of business* and defeated the challenger. Of course, this method was unhealthy, but that was how things were at the time.

So, at Mary Jo's training center, when the inner bully said, "come on, show me what you can do. You want some of this?" I did not want any of it. Mary Jo saw that something had shifted in me and moved from a willing participant to looking concerned.

"What's going on?" She asked.

"I'm feeling so sick," I said, leaning forward with eyebrows furrowed, holding my belly.

"Oh good," she replied.

"Good?" I questioned.

"Yes. You see, every time someone approaches the hidden parts hiding their divisions, they have defenses that come up. Yours is *feeling sick.*"

"How do you know this?" I asked.

"Because I have done this enough to have seen just about every pattern play out. Violence, anger, rage, sadness, hysteria… You name it, I've seen it. People can even dissociate into a version of euphoria they think of as *heavenly bliss* or some other fantastical reference in their mind. Because they are not ready for it, it doesn't last, but it can still be an extraordinary experience."

"Why doesn't it last?" I was curious as I had some of these extraordinary experiences, like being in the *womb*.

Mary Jo stood, kicked off her slippers, and danced gracefully as she answered. "Well, let's say you needed love and had an idea of what love was supposed to look and feel like." She twirled with her imaginary partner, came to a standstill, and then continued speaking. "If you perceive that you lack love and keep yourself separated from the truth of love, you will continue building evidence in your mind that you don't have it. This denial, just like the denial of a bully…"

She paused and gave me that look of knowing something about me that I hadn't ever shared with her.

"Yes, I know you, Jack. I know about the inner bully. Like the denial energy building into an interior bully, the need for love, as you've defined it, can surface in equally charged ways.

"It can look *crazy*. Perhaps you are taken to another planet in your mind and find love there. Perhaps God shows up in your life as a frog and talks to you about the meaning of life, reframing everything to make more sense for you. It will show up how it can because any denial must be healed for someone to live their wholeness. What do you say? Shall we address the bully?" She finished with a single pirouette, awaiting my answer. Mary Jo didn't mess around. She went for the jugular and it worked.

"Yes, I'm ready." I felt defeated somehow, like a kid caught with their hand in the cookie jar after being told no. She had *caught* me red-handed.

Mary Jo smiled and clapped like an excited teenager celebrating a small victory. Smoothing out her dress as she knelt, she scanned the group, centered her gaze on me, and began, "Jack, breathe and let go of resistance. In fact, everyone, let's continue this together."

The group breathed in collectively and continued connecting our breathing until we were completely in sync.

Mary Jo instructed us to lie down on meditation mats for ten minutes while continuing this conscious breathing before coming to me and asking if I was willing to trust the truth. I shook my head in agreement, and she positioned her hands purposefully, one on my forehead and the other on my abdomen. Initially, I couldn't tell what was happening. She told me later that she had been "holding space" for me to heal. In that moment, as she laid her hands on me, it felt as if she shared an extraordinary gift, something beyond my understanding, like a conduit for God's healing love.

Suddenly, an image appeared in my mind. It was of my mom and dad at the hospital on the day I was to be born. I saw myself in the womb, refusing to come out, afraid to enter this world, yet anxious to experience it at the same time. The conflict started in the womb. I had a message to share with the world. I was to tell people about Christ and was excited to do so. I also feared rejection and failure. "I know you," I heard God say to me in the womb. "I'll be with you through it all. You will succeed." And with that, I was born.

Right there, in the womb, God answered a question I hadn't known I asked. It was as if I was God, and God was me—Him, Her, It, We… all of it. God's thoughts flowed through me; they were *mine*. I came into this world with a clear purpose: to teach life skills to those who seek a genuine connection with God. Yet, for most of my life, I hid this truth from myself, fearing the persecution it might bring. To reclaim what was real, I immersed myself in reading, seeking spiritual guidance, writing, praying, and turning to professionals—therapists and healers alike. Though their support helped dissolve many internal divisions, the bully energy still lingered, unresolved, until I worked with Mary Jo.

It wasn't Mary Jo who did it, but the work she did provided an open space for people to connect with their hidden parts and integrate them back into the truth. The bully was about to be integrated and healed at long last.

"Hey, Jack, you're going to face some issues right now. I'll help." Jesus showed up, and I relaxed with his reassurance. "Many emotions will move through you. Allow them. You will feel sensations tighten and then relax. You may even feel an opening sensation followed by feelings of liquid moving through you. This is normal. Let it all happen. Trust the process. You'll be fine," he said.

"Ok," I replied. "What process?"

And then the bully showed up. "Hey, douchebag, you're going to die. You must die."

"Ask him how," Jesus prompted me.

"How?" I asked the bully.

"You will say your little prayer, and then I'm going to kill your ass," the bully replied.

Jesus continued prompting me while I focused on breathing, trusting him. "Anything else? Is that all you've got?" I asked the bully.

"Yeah, how about this? You're an awesome asshole. You have no right to abandon me." The bully's voice deepened to a penetrating tone, "You even think about it, and you'll pay."

"Thank you. Is there anything else?" I asked, feeling Jesus's presence strengthening within me. A surge of power and growing ease followed, as I watched the threats and negative emotions pass through me, dissolving as they left."

"Yes, you have an ugly life. You made this life. You think I don't see your anger? You've got a long way to go."

After letting the words and my feelings wash through me, I said quite calmly, "thank you. Is there anything else?"

"Yes, you are afraid of me, aren't you? Do you really think having your sidekick, Jesus, will save you? I will crush you."

Despite his growing aggressiveness, I continued purposefully breathing, feeling everything, listening for the truth, and then saying, "thank you. Anything else?"

"I will bust you open. I'll keep driving you to failure until you die."

"Thank you. Anything else?"

"I will cut you and tear you apart, limb from limb." That one sounded familiar.

"Thank you. Anything else?"

"I'll judge you, hate you, and break you until you despise everything about yourself."

"Thank you. Anything else?"

"I'll become every dark alley that ever terrified you, haunting you for the rest of your life."

"Thank you. Anything else?"

"I figured you'd be here with Jesus, your safety net. You wuss."

"Thank you. Anything else?"

Suddenly, the bully's temperament changed. "I want to let you in on a secret," he said. "You're free to go. You really think you can live without me? Go on then. Go create our own misery. You find a way to ruin everything anyway."

"Thank you. Anything else?"

"I want you to know how hurt I was when you left me. I want you to hear my pain. God, open Jack's ears."

And with that, my ear drum began to vibrate. It sped up so rapidly that the pain of the initial vibration settled, and I heard a voice, "Jack, you are free to go now. I was allowing you to find the truth of me in you. The nasty thoughts were traps you built to avoid pain, blocking my voice. I appreciate your willingness to face your demons and truly hear me now."

It was lovely. The voice was peaceful, and every cell in my

body resonated with love. Radiant energy flowed up and down my spine like ocean waves crashing on the shore and gently pulling back. It was incredible, and I had no questions for the voice, for I knew it was the voice I had run from as a child. Now, at peace, I simply asked, "what now?"

"Now, we will open your extrasensory senses. You will stay here for a moment and feel what is necessary to clear your body of pain."

I instantly felt anguish, and my face contorted slowly into odd positions, my throat opening as energy surged through my system. It felt like trapped energy had been stored in a large pain capacitor and suddenly released throughout my body. A sharp physical pain started in my wrist; I breathed into it until it subsided. Then, a wave of sensation flushed through my entire right side, as if fluid was flowing to different parts of my body. It was as if a crystal had liquified after standing tall for some time in its pillar of resistance. More sensations in the legs, behind my ear, and in my neck came and left.

"Now release and ask what else," I heard Jesus say.

I did, and the answer came. "It's done. You have improved your relationship with yourself immensely. You are home. Now, remain in the purity of this space and allow Christ to come out with you into the world. I did this for you, and all people are invited to go on the journey to restoration into my love. You are remembering what is true: I am. Yes, allow it. Allow life and live."

The active forces of God felt alive in me—a calming presence that centered my mind, lightened my body, and coursed through me like liquid light pouring into muscles, veins, and every fiber of my being. Mary Jo came over and said, "you're alive. And now, our class is over. Go and liven up your life. Trust this source of life that moves in you. Trust the changes that come. Like you, I have been on my journey. I will tell you; it is amazing. All the craziness will go. Be ready to live a life of awe!"

She stood, hands outstretched, reminding me of Leonardo da Vinci's Vitruvian Man. Class was over, and we were on our way. It's funny, teachers. They come into our lives and then depart, yet they often leave a mark. Some, like Mary Jo, change everything for us. No amount of money or accolades would be too much to celebrate their impact. Priceless is the truth. To all the Mary Jos out there, thank you.

But even as we celebrate them, we must remember: the real teacher always remains.

CHAPTER 7
THE LIGHT

The next morning, I awoke before Laura just at sunrise. After a short run, I made a hot latte mixed with peppermint protein and collagen powders before sitting on the patio soaking in the rays. Songbirds entertained me at the bird feeder, but besides that it was quiet.

No one knows who I am anymore. My thoughts started about the dissolution of my inner bully. *I'm not the person I was. It is as if I shed part of me that was so real to me, but it was an illusion. It's gone.*

Imagine a friend who lived in your home and did nothing but criticize you. You would be on edge and could do nothing wrong without them noticing. Now, imagine waking up one day to find the *friend* gone. Who are you without that *friend*?

No one knew me without that *friend*. I had just healed. I didn't feel that I even knew myself. Who was I with the bully gone? I had to find out and the exploration began with a question.

"Tell me, do you know my name?" I asked myself.

"Yes."

"And, what is it?"

"Jack."

"How did I get here?"

"Love." I felt myself relax into a lake of calm.

"What is love?"

"It's life eternal, always expressing itself in everything. Awareness comes to those surrendering to love. You're going to remember everything right now."

With that statement, I felt peace wash over me as my mind emptied of all chatter. I was here, on this earth, but knew not why or where to focus. *Keep your eyes on God* echoed in my head. A message from deep within my soul found its way to the surface and I had no reference for what it meant.

After all, my past would have put me on the path of going to Church, praying, or doing something to keep my eyes on God. But at that moment, I knew nothing, yet I was being informed of *something*. What that meant was a question I settled into, asking without words.

Keep your eyes on God came again. *Now raise your head and say this prayer: 'Holy Father in Heaven, can I know you completely?'*

The answer came with the question, *you already know me completely. Now, allow her face to rise to your awareness.*

With that, I saw images in my mind of women I have known: clients, my mother, my great-grandmother, and more.

People who I love are here. They have a face, and I see who they are as you see who they are. I'm asking you to see them through the eyes of Christ.

I felt a shift in my awareness as I realized what had been said. I had created images of these women from my earthly content. God was asking me to release those images and see them in a whole new light. Just as I was no longer known to anyone due to the recent changes in me, I no longer knew anyone in turn, as there was a change in how I perceived them, too. This required letting my *image* of them go, letting my judgments go, letting them be as they ARE and not as I had MADE them in my mind. Easier said than done, or was it?

"God, how do I do this?" I asked aloud. *Rest into my eyes for a moment,* I heard loud and clear. And then it happened. My vision changed from seeing with the filters I had accepted, and I began seeing as God saw these women.

My mind presented new images, showing that my great-grandfather had passed and left my great-grandmother a widow young in life. There, in my mind's eye, my great-grandfather sat in a rocking chair. A *movie* played on as I saw him smoking a pipe with great-grandma beside him.

They looked happy. With them was my grandmother who, in my previous opinion, had lived a hard life. However, now she was showing me how wonderful her life was as her kind eyes became windows into a world I hadn't known. Going back in time, for a moment I saw through her eyes while she prepared a meal. Two of her eight children played catch with a baseball in the backyard. Another set the back porch table for dinner, while two more did homework in the kitchen. She had a helper, my mom peeling potatoes. I felt warmth and compassion, love and freedom. My grandmother was happy. Scene after scene she not only showed me, but I felt her emotions and it was beautiful. A loving husband, a nurturing home, and now Heaven was her home.

After the images stopped, the comforting aura of my grandmother's warmth shifted, taking on a solemn intensity, as she urged, 'Go deeper, Jack. Look into yourself deeper. With this, I saw boats coming over from Ireland, and my great-grandmother was on one of those boats headed for Ellis Island in New York.

She was filled with hope and goodness. Her heart was pristine. Yet, when her husband died early in their marriage, he seemed to carry away her heart, leaving a hollowness in its place. Her face morphed into eyes glistening with tears ready to fall as she gazed forlornly into the distance, her head bowed with discouragement and disappointment.

A wave of profound empathy engulfed me with sadness and despair. Amidst the flood of emotion, a divine whisper reached me. *Jack, allow her heart to heal now.* And with that, my great-grandmother's young visage lifted, her gaze rising as vitality flushed her ashy cheeks and her lips parted in a breath of renewal. Before my eyes, the transformation unfolded; the sorrow in her eyes gave way to a sparkle, mirroring the restoration within her spirit. The vision of her by her husband's side evolved — she was now a beacon of love and light. Transfigured, she stood — a testament to resilience and grace. Her beingness expanded. She looked amazing.

This is how you heal, God said. *Allow yourself to become that channel through which my love can heal you in all ways. As you heal your perceptions of others, you allow my love to penetrate their consciousness. Change _how_ you see and _what_ you see will reflect the changes in you.*

I grabbed a pencil and wrote down the names of every family member I could think of. I saw them in the way of the Lord and my great-grandmother's radiance was revealed on each of them too. As the days passed, I continued this exercise, doing it with forty-five relatives, and noticed I was becoming more proficient with the process. Afterwards, I met a cousin, and our relationship felt fresh, different. It was more open and sincere. I am thankful for this practice. It has been remarkable for me, and they may be getting some benefit too.

Despite having success, a question lingered: *Why is this even needed? Didn't Jesus die for our sins? Isn't it done? Shouldn't I be perfect?* I took that question to Jesus and He had something to say about it. "Jack, the truth is I had healed every off-target thing the world taught me. There was no separation between me and Abwoon, and there never will be. However, it is a journey to get there, all of us, together. Imagine a population that knows nothing of fire. They had no heat against the cold. They had no firelight to share the stories of their clan. They had no way to cook food to prevent the spread of disease. Suddenly, fire comes on the scene. Nothing from that point forward will be the same. Suddenly, they have warmth, they have community, they have health. There is a journey to learn how to put this fire to good use, but the fire changed everything. There was one way of life before the fire and another way after.

"They were very different worlds.

"Today, if you want to cook a meal, you turn on the stove or start the grill. You still must use or apply fire to have its effect, for just bringing it into your consciousness didn't solve all your applications for fire. You have an action to take. In the early days of fire, people could have rejected it, and have nothing to do with it. But over time, the rejection of fire becomes more difficult. A car engine, a furnace, your clothes dryer, and so much more rely on the flame that brings light and heat to the world. It is impossible to ignore at some point. Likewise, is the case with me."

"Impossible to ignore, you mean?" I laughed.

"Yes. Impossible in some ways, and yet, I am still ignored plenty. However, if you want to gain the full benefits of my purpose, it would be to recognize that Christ, like fire, came into the consciousness of our world. I am someone who unlocked it and gave people access to it. I gave people insights into how to unlock the Holy Spirit in them and gain access to the active forces of God. Those insights are available to all people. Anyone can apply them, just as anyone can use fire.

When applied, the Holy Spirit brings each person through their purification process. This process is a practice that requires willingness and desire. Over time, it has become a discipline to maintain our connection with God until there is no way we can ever separate. We become conscious in that relationship. God vibrates at a certain frequency, so to speak, and your earth suit must be tuned to experience it fully.

When in that pure vibration you are in-tuned with, or one with a force of life so fantastic that no person could ever know it in its entirety. But the many *parts* of God, you being one of them, have the full capacity to know God in that part fully. That is what I bring you now. Bring you the capacity to be whole, and in that wholeness, fully express your potential. Would you like to know how to do this? If so, we're going to have a fun day."

"Yes, of course. I want nothing more," I replied to Jesus.

"Arise into God's innate being now," he said.

With his words, I closed my eyes and could see a village, and then I was lifted into the sky, watching the earth move further and further away. "Where are we?" I asked Jesus.

"This is a command post of sorts. I brought you here to show you a picture of humanity from my perspective—the perspective of Christ. Take a moment to look around."

I zoomed in on Papua New Guinea, then to Australia, New Zealand and Argentina. My travels continued around the globe in less than a minute. I saw lights at various stages of illumination where populations existed. My second pass around the world took several minutes, and this time, I was shown individuals and groups with very bright luminescence. Their field of light spread for miles and miles with rays firing off to other parts of the world. They were like suns, radiating life and love.

"That one," Jesus pointed to one of the brightest lights, "has helped 10,000 people find our Lord through comedy. She was once a dim light; most people had written her off as a lost cause. However, one day her mother-in-law prayed for her and, as a result, a message was sent to a florist who had a rototiller in her back trunk. She was to deliver the rototiller to a park and leave it there. Confused, the florist followed this divine spark and dropped it off on a Thursday. That night, our lost cause had a dream to pick up the rototiller at the park. She ignored the message. Friday before falling to sleep she asked God to show her a path for her life. The same dream happened Friday night. She ignored it but was curious. Saturday afternoon, her brother called and asked if she wanted to go for a drive.

"After four hours of digging in the garden, he complained about his back and needed a break. She agreed and he picked her up. Halfway through the drive, she noticed her surroundings looked familiar and saw a sign for the park from her dream. 'Can we go there?' She asked and her brother obliged. The park was empty, but a rototiller was next to the sign. 'Oh, my God, that was in my dream!' She exclaimed. 'That is for us!'

"Exploring the rototiller, *randomly* dropped off at a park, she noticed a sticker for the Second City comedy club in Chicago reading 'Call me if you are funny', and Bill Murray signed it. Long story short, she called the number and started a career. Her brother saved his back with a powerful rototiller, and at least 10,000 people have turned to God. She is a light helping some of the darker lights find their way."

"Wow, that is an incredible story!" I exclaimed.

"Yes, it is. The mountains of stories I could share would fill your soul for an eternity."

I marveled at the one story and was curious about what happened with the florist. "The florist doesn't know, does she?"

"No, she doesn't," he replied. "But, three days later, a massive floral contract arrived from a friend I trust with big things. Our florist friend could have bought one hundred rototillers with the contract if she liked. It is a great day when someone is aligned, Jack. Good things tend to happen."

After this story, I saw the lights differently. They weren't just lights but represented the active forces of God in motion. It was quite a spectacle.

"You see, Jack," Jesus informed me, "everyone who has ever lived has a light. Some have turned away from God so much that they rely on the lights of others to navigate their life. They focus very much on the world and depend on others for their perception. The dimmer the light, the more co-dependent their relationships.

"The brighter ones have found a source of light, that Source connection within themselves, and are in various states of refinement to know God more fully. The brightest lights are like the sun in your world. They can teach others how to access the light within themselves. In doing so, they are one with the source of God and bring pure love to situations. I teach these people directly. They will do what it takes to support the ultimate vision put in motion when I was here."

"Why hasn't that vision happened yet?" I asked.

"It has in the spirit. It is unfolding now in the world with each passing day. You'll see. I want to show you something. I would like you to see what happens when everyone's lights are on when collectively the world knows itself as God knows Itself." Jesus lifted his hands together above his head and opened them quickly.

The scene completely changed into one massive ball of light and I could no longer see the individual outlines of people even if I zoomed in. The light appeared to have no beginning or end. It was alive, and more beautiful than anything I'd seen. Remember the first time you saw a massive bonfire? Remember how much awe you felt at the incredible site. That times a million might give a sense of how amazing this was.

"Jesus, what am I looking at? Is the earth even still down there? All I see is light."

"Yes, it's still there, but it has transformed as the people have. Nothing is as it was. Imagine the earth before cities existed—no buildings, restaurants, gas stations, or roads. If I had shown you what could be created when nothing modern existed, you would have been blown away, right? You'll have to trust me that the world is changing magnificently, and it will usher in an age when no one goes hungry. Jack, I am the bread of life. Anyone who comes to me will not hunger. As you have seen here, their light will illuminate fully, and your current world will transform into this." His hands reached out through space, appearing to hold the earth in his palms.

"So, they have to believe in you?" I asked, realizing this vision would take lifetimes, perhaps even eons.

"They live as Christ, and the rest is history," he replied, making it sound so simple.

"But they don't know how. Some of them don't even know what Christ is. There is a war on religion, a war on people. There is so much division. How do you expect this to happen? How is it even possible to have your vision realized."

I felt frustration, anger, and fear that it wouldn't happen. I had been one of those people lost in the darkness and viewed myself as lucky that I had transformed, but it was only after my crisis. *How could that happen with so many people? Impossible*, I thought.

As if hearing my thoughts, Jesus said, "Jack, you don't have to do it. God's got this. Trust the process. Everyone will have an opportunity to return *home*. Within everyone is an invitation to return. God's got this."

REFLECT & CONNECT
Chapters 5-7

Before moving forward, pause to reflect on your journey so far.

CH. 5: Exploring Denial: Denial is described as a powerful force keeping Jack from wholeness. Are you willing to witness (no judgment) how denial shows up for you? Take moment to consider how denial is operating in your life.

CH. 6: Seeing Through a Divine Lens: Jack's experience opens an "extrasensory" awareness, allowing him to perceive more spiritually. Have you had moments when you felt more connected to the unseen, expansive divine reality? How did this change your perspective?

CH. 7: The Power of Ancestral Healing: Jack's visions allow him to heal perceptions of his ancestors. How do you think understanding and healing family stories or patterns can impact your own growth?

DIVE DEEPER - Join the conversation. Explore more thought-provoking questions and share your insights inside the **O Coalition Portal**.

Scan the QR Code to Enter the Discussion

thelowlyprophet.com/ tlp-reflect&connect

NEXT STEP
Walk the path. Live the transformation.

Continue Your **Transformational Journey.** Integrate these incredible tools into your daily life.

Scan to Apply TOOL 3 and
Release Attachments that No Longer Serve You.

thelowlyprophet.com/tlp-nextstep

TOOL 3: Perception Correction

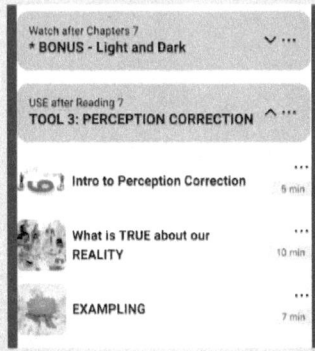

1. Locate TOOL 3 in the Syllabus

2. Watch, Read, and Practice the exercises.

3. Use the exercises **WHILE** reading Chapters 8 & 9

Objective: You will cultivate a steady and reliable connection to Creative and Divine Intelligence. This means accessing inspiration, wisdom, and intuitive insights with greater ease and consistency in your daily life.

CHAPTER 8
HEALING CRAZY

M y frustration was high. *Why couldn't we have everything peaceful and perfect in our world today? Why did God create a place with so many obstacles to realizing its potential? What the heck was going on in God's mind that we have to endure so much dysfunction? Shouldn't people know how to do what is right? Shouldn't they know what is in the highest and best*

interests of our world? Dammit all. I felt rage and shame: Rage that the world *should be* perfect already and shame that I hadn't done more to help God manifest this magnificent plan of perfection held in my mind.

Wrangling about this one evening, Jesus showed up on my doorstep. As I opened my door, I felt like I was stepping back in time.

"Hey, Jack, I want to take you for a ride. Let's go have some fun." He was dressed for a party as if it were the early 1930s in downtown Chicago. His top hat in hand revealed black, slicked back hair, a pencil thin mustache and NO beard!

"Is that you, Jesus?" I yelped. "Did you really shave?"

That wasn't the only thing new. The tunic was replaced with a tailored charcoal and white pinstripe suit, and He fit in with the décor of the scenery behind him that included a black Packard 734 Speedster.

"Some trick, Jesus. How did you do this? Never mind. How should I dress?" I looked down anticipating my pajama top and bottoms, but as you might have guessed, I was also dressed to party in my own blue three-piece suit. I looked a lot like him minus the obvious glow that accompanied him everywhere. "Ok, I guess I'm ready."

We drove downtown and parked near an old liquor store. It was still prohibition, but Jesus *knew a guy*. We entered a back alley and through a doorway labeled *Laundromat*. "Let me do the talking," Jesus said. I did, and soon we had a table near the dance floor. Jesus ordered some wine and told me to relax.

"You know this is illegal, right?" I was aware of my history enough to understand prohibition in the early 1930s.

"Yes, I know, but we needed to come here for your behalf, Jack. Trust me. Let's get some food." Jesus did his best to create some normalcy amidst the unusual circumstances. The place was buzzing; a jazz ensemble blared, and two young ladies in flapper outfits leaped up to do the jitterbug, encouraging their dates to join in. Jesus smiled as he turned back to me, saying, "You know, when I was a young boy, my father told me I could do a lot with my life. He said I had a gift for carpentry. I did, but I wanted more than what carpentry could offer. I couldn't have known my Father in Heaven had I avoided my life mission. I could have and would have made a good life as a career carpenter, but not a great life. I had a great life, my friend."

"Yeah, until you were murdered at the ripe age of too young to die." I retorted in words clipped with disdain. Even as I spoke, I heard my own fear of persecution in my voice.

"That's not the way I see it," Jesus said with a smirk, "though it was not pleasant being nailed to that cross."

"How do you see it?" I asked. I felt a blush creep into my cheeks. "I mean, that had to be bad."

"The way I see it is a lot like this bar." Jesus looked around, motioning with his hands so that I could observe the scene. "No one knows what's inside the *laundromat* until they open that door. They may have been told it's a speakeasy, they may even know someone who's been here, but there's no way they can be sure until they come in, sit down and participate. This is why I called you to join me. I need you to see what is happening in your life. You entered into a new world of Christ. Some people think they know Jesus, but they don't know me. They know *about* me. Some people think they know Christ, and they may know about the one called Jesus the Christ, but they haven't opened the *laundromat* door to experience Christ. I want you to bring people to the speakeasy for today's generations and help people experience Christ."

I got it. There it was, a mission beyond my abilities brought to my attention with nowhere to hide. Silent momentarily, I prayed and then said, "there is nothing more I want to do than that. But how? I don't know how to bring people to 1930s Chicago and have this type of trippy experience."

"I know. I know. This is for you. You will have revealed how to share Christ's true nature. Trust me. I just needed you to really get it at a deeper level, and I thought this charade would do the trick. How am I doing?" He asked with a confident smile.

"I get it," I said. "Now what?"

"Now we enjoy our meals, dance a little, and then you can address your anger, heal what is actually going on with you. Are you ready?"

"Sure." I muttered. I was unenthusiastic because this inner work took time, and I'd hoped for a simple answer. *This could take forever.* I was still so angry, believing God should have made this whole thing easier. I didn't understand, but I realized it was time for me to heal.

After dancing, I closed my eyes and instantly found myself back at home, in my pajamas, stewing over God. I wanted answers.

While sitting on my living room couch, I fell into a dream-like state where God revealed my life as a two-dimensional figure. From the front, I looked just like me. From the side, I looked like a line. There needed to be depth. He showed me my third-grade gym class in two dimensions, which was confusing and pointless. He then said, "Jack, this universe has three dimensions for a reason."

Without saying a word, God changed the world back to three dimensions, but this time there was no gravity. Not only did the people (and everything else) float off into space and die, but the earth couldn't hold itself together and began to disappear. "Jack, the earth has gravity for a reason." This went on for a while as God showed me the reasons for insects (life would cease to exist without them) and many other things I hated about life on Earth.

Next, I was shown my life events—especially the ones I

hated most. I saw the disappointment on my father's face as he comforted my toddler sister, who nearly drowned because I slipped down an incline to the deep end of a hotel pool. Thankfully, he was there to save the day. I experienced the shame of filming myself naked and my parents finding the tape. Some events taught me how to treat people well. Some taught me the value of money. Others taught me about love, honesty, trust, and faith.

Ready to move on, God then showed me how the effects of denial led to mental illness and how my own mental illness was an outcome of that denial. There I was in fifth grade religion class discussing the death penalty. So many of my classmates wanted the criminals to die. I agreed in order to be accepted, but I really wanted everyone to live. Denial. I often felt stupid and ill-equipped for playground conversations around sports, girls, music and more. To feel included, I'd lie about seeing the big game, or who I had a crush on, or whether I had heard of the latest hot band. Denial.

"Are you ok?" A friend would ask as I was clearly in distress. "Oh, sure, I'm fine." Denial.

"Have you ever done this before?"

"Who did you vote for?"

"Did you kiss?"

"Were you afraid?"

The list went on and on and I saw how I dissociated and blocked the truth until I was deaf, blind, and dumb spiritually. I had cut off life to God telling me what was true because I had cut off life to the truth in me. Denial.

God then said I could heal my mental illness and showed me how.

I saw every part of the mental illness dismantled until my brain was healthy again. All around me, images of life events rapidly rose up, and those moments changed as I chose to release the lies, feel the pain, and allow the unwinding of the past until the imagery stopped and my focus shifted from those past events toward a future filled with love and light. He told me this was my path. He said I would be healthy. I believed. My eyes opened with a smile on my face and peace in my heart. Anger had lifted. I saw the reason behind everything: To invite me to choose God. It was perfect, it really was, and I had work to do.

CHAPTER 9
A PREPARED HOME - TERESA

Determined to live fully in Christ, I spent countless hours meditating, praying, learning, and applying what I learned daily. Before long, people began to refer others to me for spiritual guidance. One such referral was Teresa.

There was nothing spectacular about Teresa, in fact, she might have been called a plain Jane by some. Embarrassment about a significant birthmark on her left thigh caused her to do whatever possible to hide in plain sight. Despite feeling insecure about it, she felt unique after reading that people with birthmarks may have past lives where they died from physical wounds in those areas. Birthmarks, so the claim went, served as reminders in their new lives of unhealed traumas.

Though Teresa didn't believe in past lives, she had a recurring childhood dream of dying suddenly underwater, awakening in tears holding her left leg. Teresa, now in her mid-thirties, went through an incredible transformation while working with me and promised to share her experiences on a podcast intended to spread hope to others through incredible stories. Though her story is not about healing *past-life* trauma, it is compelling.

On recording day, Teresa's purple yoga pants and oversized gold sweatshirt mirrored the podcast studio's casual vibe. Sound-proofing foam decorated the walls, and an empty wood grain table with mounted mics separated Teresa from the host. I listened in from a waiting room. The host got comfortable, opened the show, and invited Teresa to share her story. She leaned into the microphone and began:

TERESA

"When I was young, I had a ball, a favorite ball. It was black with a green stripe. I carried it everywhere until I lost it. For years, I thought about that ball, revisiting where it possibly might be. I would even look for it again, though it was long gone. This had me in knots at times, turmoil over a ball. Can you imagine? You may think this is silly, but perhaps there is something you hang onto that no longer exists in your life, except in your mind, perhaps even in your cells. It is tortuous. My name is Teresa, and this is my story."

Jack came to me in the hospital and told me I could heal. I had checked myself in due to overwhelming anxiety. He casually shared his story and then told me I could heal, too. No one had ever said to me that I could live a healthy life. I believed him and asked if he would work with me. That first session was awesome.

I remember he said, "Teresa, allow trusting yourself for a moment. Let your mind bring up what is in your highest and best interests to heal." Jack got right into it.

After thinking for a moment, a memory shot up, an experience I wish I could forget. It was in high school. I had agreed to drink with some friends and was on cloud nine. I had been accepted by a group that I cared for incredibly. But that night, after drinking too much, I blacked out. The next day I woke up sick to my stomach. Something had happened, but I couldn't remember what. My friend told me coldly that it would be best if I went home. Everything felt off. Noticing my emotions rising, Jack interrupted my story.

"Right there. Stop and feel what you are feeling. Stay with it." He encouraged me.

I did stay with it. Images from that night flashed before my eyes and waves of emotions came and left. It was hard to sit there in the pain but, for the first time ever, I did. I stayed with it, not trying to fix it like I had in the past, but feeling and witnessing what arose through me. At some point, there was a shift, and the image of that black and green striped ball came to the surface. I saw the connection of trying to figure out what happened to that ball just as I was trying to figure out what happened that night in high school. I let go of the ball and allowed it to be lost and gone. I released it for good. I released trying to change what happened in high school and allowed it to be as it was. I let go of beating myself up and allowed Christ to see what I had tried to hide.

Once doing so, another wave of emotion swept through me. I healed. I healed. Jack asked me to return to the memory and let any remaining insights come forward. As I did, I tuned into a thought that I should be sinful in order to be saved. That I needed to be a *bad girl* in order to be saved from myself.

I was taught at a very young age that we are born broken. I wanted to get that sin out of me and push it onto the world, so it no longer tortured my mind. I didn't know how to heal it. I needed help. Jack saw this and created a space for it to come out healthily. I wrote down all the reasons I was bad and let the emotions come out with the writing. At the end, I saw the list and laughed at how silly my actions were.

As I laughed, Jack encouraged me. "This is how it works, Teresa. We hold onto the sins or the things that are against God and we harbor them in hidden places within us. Despite hiding them, they carry with them a resonant frequency. That frequency attracts matching experiences to bring any hidden parts into the light, to the surface of our minds. When nothing remains hidden, there is a clean *house* if you will.

"When you are purified in this way, you make room for God to live in that *home* and your life becomes very different. You will find everything you need to heal. You will be attracted to the right doctors, the right medicines, nutrients, practices, and all the rest. You might even attract someone like me to help you spiritually align things. You are well on your way to health, Teresa."

He was right too. As I let the hidden parts within me surface, everything changed. Slowly, at first, but rather quickly over time. I hid from self-hate and pretended to be Ms. Perfect because I couldn't stand the possibility of being as awful as I thought I was.

I recall judging my sister for hating my mom. She sat on the stairs crying as our dad told her it was not ok being hateful towards Mom. He was furious. I wanted to defend her but I was so young. I hated that he crushed my sister emotionally like that. He was so big and powerful. My sister was fragile and shut down. I vowed never to let him get to me that way, but he did, and I hated myself for that. If I could heal that hate, I could heal anything. I brought it to Jack. He told me to give myself permission to feel the hate. I did, and this is what happened:

"I feel a sensation of burning in my throat, almost like acid reflux and now I feel my eyes closing tightly as if I don't want to see what it is I'm looking for. I'm scared."

"It's ok, Teresa," Jack reassured me. "Trust the process."

I stayed with the sensations, and my system went from relaxed to tense and back to relaxed. I was somehow cutting through the layers of this awful *cake* I had baked. I saw my sister (in my mind) helpless, and Jack told me to talk with her.

"Look her in the eyes, Teresa, and open your heart. Allow the words and actions you want to give her to come forth," he instructed.

I did this, clearly talking with my sister in my imagination, and said, "I know you are hurting. Dad is mad. He's trying to protect Mom and feels guilty for not being around to help more. He thinks this is helping. He doesn't know how scared you are. Can I hug you? You'll be ok." She nodded yes and we hugged in my mind, but it felt so real. I instantly started balling and my arms wrapped around myself. I was the one who held in that pain, not my sister and not my dad. I was the one hurting from failing to save my sister from pain. I felt worthless, and ill-equipped, and couldn't stand that I failed someone I loved and cared for. At that moment, the emotions poured out from me, and before I knew it the crying stopped. I felt peaceful. With my sister's eyes on me, Jack prompted me again.

"Teresa, ask your sister if she wants anything."

I did and she *said*, "I forgive you, Teresa," and another wave of emotion flowed through me as shame and guilt finally released.

"Thank you. Is there anything else?" I asked her.

"Yes, you're free now. I am leaving. Thanks for bringing love to this and releasing it. You're free." And, with that, she was gone. I smiled and laughed. I faced the hate in me and felt free of it for the first time in a long time, perhaps since childhood. I tried for years to get rid of the shame by covering it with hate. It wasn't that I was a hateful person, but had held onto vengeance in my heart to protect myself from perceiving my failure at being a *good sister*.

As this unfolded, Jack suggested I release my perceptions and definitions of 'good sister'. I did by saying, "I release trying to pretend to be a good sister. I cancel my need to uphold a false image of a *good sister*. I let go of trying to manage expectations of people and their perceptions of me. I allow them to see me how they see me, whatever type of sister they see. And, I invite Love, the Love of Christ to heal anything in the way of me living in perfect harmony as God created me to be. Holy Spirit, clear out any denial in me, allow love to be my present state, and may I act from this point forward from love. Thank you. Thank you. Thank you. Jack, thank you too." I concluded.

He smiled knowing the peace in me was real.

Jack became my coach for some time. He never tried to fix anything, but just showed up and allowed me to go where I needed to, supporting my clearing anything in the way of allowing God to mold me in Its image and make a home within me. Today marks two years since working with Jack, and I feel great. I'm off all but one of my medications, have access to resources I hadn't known prior to working with him, and feel confident I am on the wellness side of my mental illness. I am free of so much pain, and more healing is on its way. I can feel it. I want everyone to know how a simple change can lead to massive changes in their lives. You don't HAVE to heal, but you likely will. I believe our natural state is healthy, and that is a state everyone can pursue if they are willing.

As I listened to Teresa sharing her story, I recalled the past several months with her. She worked through traumas, stories, beliefs, ideals, misunderstandings, faith distortions, false narratives, and stored treasures she falsely held sacred in her mind. She returned to a binary understanding of being pure in her spirit versus disturbing that purity. Her soul had healed, and that is what I enjoy doing the most, helping people return to the center, that place where God meets us, if we allow it. If Teresa previously had a messy house where guests weren't welcomed or comfortable, her *house* had been readied for the most special guest of all, our Beloved Creator. *Now, we begin...*

Just as the thought crossed my mind, I looked up and saw the interviewer waving me into the studio to explore my version of events. I began, "health has been available since Teresa was able to do what I asked."

Curious, the interviewer followed up with, "what do you mean by *able to* and what were you asking her to do?"

I answered, "if you have a dirty kitchen with dishes all over the counter and slop in the sink, you are not able to prepare a meal properly. When you take the time to clean and prepare, you are able to address what happens in your house more easily. Then, if a friend stops by, you can have them in for a coffee.

"When a meal is to be prepared, you are ready to begin without much trouble. Teresa prepared her *house* for the one guest she cared about. That guest will only come into a prepared *home*. I asked Teresa to prepare for that guest. Success was certain for her the moment she chose to say yes. That *yes* was to herself, a willingness that is always required for any of this to be effective. Her continued discipline maintaining that prepared state is necessary for her best life."

"What do you expect to happen next for Teresa?" The interviewer asked.

"I expect her to live as a Christ in this world. And anytime Christ is in the world, that is a great day."

The interviewer was taken aback by my response. But Teresa and I just smiled as we could sense the podcast host would soon be called as well.

REFLECT & CONNECT
Chapters 8 & 9

Before moving forward, pause to reflect on your journey so far.

CH. 8: What obstacles or frustrations in your life feel "unfair" or "wrong"? How might seeing these obstacles through God's eyes—understanding their deeper purpose—change your perception of them?

CH. 9: How can you invite love and forgiveness into areas of your life where shame or guilt still linger? Teresa's journey of releasing shame involved bringing hidden feelings to the surface. What areas of your life need this same type of attention and forgiveness?

DIVE DEEPER - Join the conversation. Explore more thought-provoking questions and share your insights inside the **O Coalition Portal**.

Scan the QR Code to Enter the Discussion

thelowlyprophet.com/ tlp-reflect&connect

NEXT STEP
Walk the path. Live the transformation.

The most transformative lesson on Words you may ever come by. It allows you to purify deceptions and renew life!!!

BONUS: WORDS

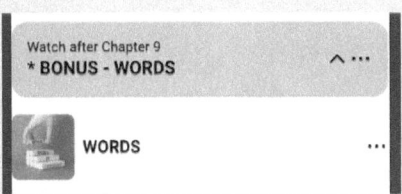

1. Locate BONUS - WORDS in the Syllabus

2. Listen, Read, and Practice the exercises.

3. Use the exercises as you read.

Objective: You will release personal projections and emotional charges attached to words, allowing them to return to their true, neutral essence. Instead of defining words based on past experiences or emotions, you will experience them as they are—free from personal bias or distortion.

Scan to Purify Words in Your Life with BONUS: WORDS

thelowlyprophet.com/tlp-nextstep

CHAPTER 10
MIRACLES

Nothing invigorates me more than working with clients. One morning, after a third session at my desk, I got up to relax on the office couch. Sitting with my eyes closed, I focused on my breath and felt the power of love surge through me. I imagine a smartphone would feel this way when plugged into an outlet after a day of use. During the fifteen-minute process, I tuned into God and asked if Jesus could help me with something.

"*Jesus, are you there?*" I asked in my mind.

"Yes," the response came instantly.

"Jesus, would you help me open up the fruits of this life more fully?" I was incredibly interested in the miracles that now seemed to come more frequently. I was curious if I could control them rather than just witness them.

"Jack, what are you asking?" Jesus replied.

"I guess I want to know how to make a miracle happen. You know, like you did."

"Like I did?" Jesus asked, smiling.

"Yes. The healing of the leper, for example. Why don't I have that same ability to heal a leper?"

Looking around, Jesus laughed and said, "besides the fact that lepers aren't around here?"

"You know what I mean. I want to perform miracles like you did."

"Jack, you are performing miracles like I did. Don't you see that?"

"I haven't done anything, Jesus. I just surrender and God seems to do things through me. It is awesome. Don't get me wrong. It's incredible. But I want to be more in command of the miracles. I don't feel like I'm in control at all. God will have me say something to a person and it happens to be supportive of them healing a division in their spirit, and the outcomes are stupendous. That's cool, but I perceive you were better at it than I am; that it came easier to you. I want to learn more from you."

"Oh, I see," Jesus replied. "You think I could wave a magic wand and have stuff happen? Is that it?"

"Well, yes? I guess so, minus the magic wand."

He fell silent and I hoped he was preparing to teach what I asked. Instead, he gently leaned in saying, "that's not how it works, Jack."

"Then how does it work?" Though it happened more than I care to admit, Jesus always corrected false perceptions.

He paused and in my mind's eye, he took out a marker. "If I used this marker and wrote on a piece of paper, what would you think?"

I shared the first thing that came to mind. "That you wrote on a piece of paper, but I wouldn't know what to really think until I saw what you wrote."

"Right. But what if you didn't have context about markers? What if you had never seen a writing instrument of this nature? What if the only writing you had seen was in black ink, but my marker wrote in red? Then what would you think?"

"I would be in awe. It would be a..."

Jesus finished my sentence, "...miracle?"

"I suppose, yes," I replied. Wow, is he good!

"But if you already know about red markers, you won't be focused on the red marker as fascinating, but on how I used the red marker, right?"

"Ok. Yes. I'm tracking with you."

"My turning water to wine is the *red marker applied* to a situation that blew people away. They didn't know that was possible, and I will tell you something. Your ability to support someone in healing a mental illness by reconnecting them with our source of love, God, is a modern-day miracle. However, you know how it works. You have a red marker in a world where most people have never seen a red marker. That is all. In my time, it was important to show the mystical powers of God in a way to fulfill the scriptures.

"Through me, God brought forth a tool to bring about transformation for people stuck in a framework that was tribal. My life interrupted their thinking by showing the *impossible* and opening them to new ideas. That was quite a trip for people, let me tell you. But I knew what was happening. It wasn't as much of a mystery to me. I knew. I was in awe, but I knew." He let that settle in for a moment before asking me, "you don't have a clue how to create an electric car do you?"

"No, not a clue."

"But, you believe you can have an all-electric car, yes?"

"If I had the money and interest, yes," I answered.

"But go back in time to 1900 and imagine an auto mechanic being told that in the future, automobiles will be run by electricity. What would he say?"

Playing along, I answered, "I'm pretty sure the mechanic would have laughed. I actually studied this, and electric cars at that time were more like parlor tricks than anything sustainable. I doubt he would have imagined electric cars being the way to go."

While drawing a line representing time, Jesus shared, "somewhere along the way, though, someone gained enough understanding of battery technologies and automobiles to create something once deemed unlikely, if not impossible. What changed?" he asked.

"The belief that it was possible and the desire to have it," I said.

"And what fueled those?" he prompted.

"Well, the desire came from God. And the belief came from education, experience, and a place of faith."

"Precisely, Jack. One night in the dream states of curious engineers, there erupted solutions to all the issues related to battery-run automobiles, and voila, they were viable."

"Well, it didn't happen in one night, did it?" I asked, assuming he wasn't giving the literal history.

"No, not in your timeline. But, in the spirit, the process of desire instantaneously produces everything needed to bring it into manifestation. And similarly to the automobile story, there was a plan for me to come to the planet and awaken something real in people to reconnect directly with our God, a God who desires us to know It fully in all its feminine, masculine, ethereal, dimensional, physical, and energetic aspects. God wanted people to rise from their slumber and reconnect with It, know It, and shift attention from the separate perspective of being small and isolated to the whole perspective of God as one with them. And guess what? I was the *engineer* who woke from the dream with the understanding that I and my Father were one. Just like the engineer in the early days of battery-powered cars, I was the only one who believed it. But over time I won over converts to see it as I saw it and they helped me spread the word."

"Oh my. I get it. So, you believed it and knew it to be true."

"Yes, I did, well before evidence in the world proved it."

"How did you know?" I asked.

"The same way you knew how to help Teresa and all the others you have been working with."

Suddenly, my perspective of Jesus, the human being, having always known everything all at once, collapsed as I reflected on how I'd known to help Teresa. "I went crazy, Jesus. I know how to help because you taught me how to come out of insanity. I learned through immersion in a situation that was untenable, and against all odds as far as the world knew."

"Right, but when did you know that you would be well? After all, a prestigious doctor very clearly said your brain was like a broken computer motherboard, and you needed medicine to be the glue to hold you together." His question caught me off guard and I went back through my memories to think about it. One image stood out.

"I knew in that first hospitalization that I would get well. I knew the first time they told me I was crazy that I was going to heal completely."

"And did you ever have doubts?"

"Yes, I did. There were some very challenging moments and I doubted many times, especially when medications were changed, another hospitalization happened, or a solution I invested in failed. After failing to get well multiple times, I wondered if my doctors were right. I wondered if I suffered from delusions of grandeur and would be stuck in a fantasy world only I could see."

"And how did you move through your doubts?" He asked.

"Honestly, I prayed. I asked God to show up and guide every step of that way. Lost of my own volition, I leaned on Divine guidance. And every time it came through. I didn't always see it in the moment, but hindsight was helpful. Over time, I learned to trust that God's way would lead me to healing. It was incredible. And though I didn't always see evidence of healing as quickly as I wanted, I persisted. Piled-up milestones helped me notice I was getting well until I was fully healthy." In my own story, I was seeing the wisdom in Jesus's handholding.

"You see," Jesus said enthusiastically, "that is exactly how I came to know myself as the Christ. You are Jack the Christ, and millions of Christs will be *born* in the coming years. And in Christ, the only begotten son of God, you will realize God loves all of His, Her, Its creations. She loves them by breathing life into them. He loves them by giving them free will. It loves infinitely for It is the truth of love. And you were created from the same substance of our God in the form of a human being, with the programming all built in to awaken as Christ. That alone will heal mental illness on your planet. Do you believe this?"

"Of course. You know I do. I don't know why, but I know it." An excitement and sense of expansiveness opened in me.

"Now we're talking," Jesus said. "That is the attitude I had when I began my ministry. I knew. Over time, God revealed to me the end was coming for me, that I had little time left. I made every moment count and stayed in tune with God even when the world pulled on me to make its way more important. Not everyone is going to like the changes in you.

"There are people who will want you to stay the *caterpillar*, for that is the one they know, the one they are comfortable with. Some will call you crazy, for the only Christ that is possible for them is Jesus the Christ. You'll have to learn to maintain your presence as a Christ even when under attack. Remember when I told Peter to 'get behind me Satan.' I rebuked him to make my priorities clear and reinforce in me who I served. Anyone who lives as a Christ eventually only serves the one true God. But until then, there is work to do in clearing out anything standing in the way of that."

"What do you mean?" I asked. "You said 'Christ <u>eventually</u> only serves God'. Doesn't Christ <u>always</u> serve only God?"

"Jack, you have some work to do still. There are elements in you that still lean toward sin and you will need to clean those up. Think of it this way. Have you had an off day?"

"Yes, of course."

"And when you had the off day, did you automatically turn to be in a relationship with God?"

"No, of course not. I've turned to worldly distractions plenty of times."

"Like what?"

"Does it matter?" I replied, thinking of the hour and a half I spent on social media the night before.

"No. Whatever it is, if it is what you turned to instead of God, you shifted from the Christ centered being to the disconnected non-being, even if for a moment. I want to see you release all distractions and make God the first focus of your attention. That will be when your true ministry begins. And that day is coming. Keep at it. By the way, Jack, when you turn to God first, there will still be time for movies, friends, parties, sports, and more. These activities, however, will align with love and support your mission rather than distract from it."

"But how do I do that?"

"You'll see. Just as you've shed mountains of distractions from your life already, so you'll shed the rest. You will be purified until the Christ is all you can be. Right now, you are still bouncing back and forth. You used to be in that Christ space no more than five minutes before running away from it. That was ok, because you couldn't stand seeing your issues in that light. Now, you can sustain being in that light for quite some time and it is rare that you bounce out of it. I know you can see the difference. And what is your life like in that Christ awareness?"

It's so tough to put into words, but I tried. "It's magical, wonderful, glorious. I continue to experience awe at how amazing it is. No comparison. My life outside of Christ is empty and in Christ, I feel fulfilled even before I take any action. Results come quicker and my stress is lower. I suppose the example of the caterpillar and butterfly applies. As the caterpillar, I knew life one way and it was fine. It was all I knew. But the butterfly opens a whole new world, literally. Instead of learning how to fly like a butterfly, I have learned to help people find their center and choose to live there more and more in alignment with God. I get to witness the great unwinding of errors in people as they transform to live their best lives."

"Yes. Yes. Yes." Jesus grinned as he touched his nose playfully and pointed at me, laughing with excitement.

I was getting it, and I couldn't wait to get it more.

CHAPTER 11
THE GARDEN

For many reasons, the farmer's market is a favorite Saturday morning pastime. Cool early mornings, sunshine, hot coffee, happy people, fresh food, and on this occasion, organic seeds. It was springtime and, for the first time in years, my wife wanted to build a vegetable garden. Recent shortages at the grocery store had spooked her, and she wanted to learn how to grow our own food just in case.

Our first attempt, in early marriage, could have been better. The squirrels and bunnies ate more from our garden than we did, but we were determined to do it right this time.

After a day's work preparing our new garden, we both rested on the grass. Dirty as possible, we sipped Pina Coladas, which a neighbor brought by on her way to a social gathering. Laura and I laughed at the irony of our life. We had been through a tumultuous time early in our marriage with the loss of a baby, and over Pina Coladas, we had decided to build a house and have a home that was all prepared for our future family.

We placed a special emphasis on our imagined garden sprouting all types of mystical foods that would cure any ailment, including miscarriages. Now, here we were many years later, building a garden and sipping Pina Coladas once again. We had no mystical foods to plant, and thankfully had our kids so we went for the basics this time, carrots, potatoes, tomatoes, green beans, and lettuce would have to do.

"Jack, do you remember that story you told me about the seeds? The one Jesus... well, you know."

Laura thought my conversations with Jesus were in my head. She didn't in the least believe my relationship with him was real. For a while this frustrated me, but then I realized it also must be part of God's plan. Her memory of me thinking I was Jesus during a manic episode still carried a lot of pain with it. She knew I wasn't in that place anymore but had no interest in feeling it again. She did like the seed story, though.

"Yes, hon, I remember it."

"Would you tell it to me?" Laura asked.

Something was going on here. She never asked me to tell her stories about Jesus. Perhaps this was part of her healing. Perhaps she wanted to have a relationship with him. Perhaps it was her saying, *I love you, no matter what.*

"Ok, honey, I'll share it." I took a deep breath and closed my eyes, leaning back supported by my hands resting in the grass. It was around 4 pm and the sun provided just enough warmth to enjoy this perfect afternoon.

"Everything in life begins as a seed," I started, "and that seed has within it everything it needs to become what is possible for it. The apple seed has the potential to become an apple tree. It will never be a pear tree, but it can become a great apple tree. It is in the design of the seed. If that seed is given the right conditions, it will become an apple tree. It also has the potential to remain a seed and never grow an inch.

"Christ is the same way—the potential for a person to live as Christ is available. The *seed* exists in you, and Jesus told us how to activate this and have it grow and mature into what is possible for every person. In its early days, it will require a lot of TLC, just as the apple tree would. As time goes on, that apple tree produces fruit, and likewise, so does Christ. His or her *fruit* will show up as something God wishes to bring into that part of the world, which is always good. To the untrained eye, a tree is a mystery before it produces fruit.

"Will this tree produce apples, pears, oranges, bananas, or nuts? However, a tree's potential is known to the trained eye long before it produces fruit. And so it is with being another Christ. A person's potential is known in its early stages and those in the world with trained eyes will come to support a person reaching his or her potential. They can't change a person's gift from one thing to another, just as the farmer can't change an apple tree into a pear tree. However, a person who sees the potential in another can support that person in recognizing and accepting their gifts, their talents, the truth of who they are to become."

I looked over at Laura. Her face glistened in the sun, her head held back, her eyes closed, and soaking in the story. "What if the apple tree didn't like itself though? What if it withered and shrank from its potential, judging that it was a bad tree and unworthy of producing good fruit?

"Of course, you and I know that an apple tree is an apple tree no matter what it thinks of itself. But the effect of judging itself shuts down its systems, cutting off essential nutrients resulting in a tragedy, no fruit. An intervention supports the apple tree in letting go of its false perceptions so it can step fully into what is possible. People do this all the time. They judge and shut down the faculties available for their life to fully come online, for their potential to be realized.

"When a person denies who they are, their interests, their worth, and judges themselves without a way to unwind those errors, that person withers and shrinks into darkness, failing to produce its *fruit*. That person is not as alive as they could be. But it is possible to change this. It is possible to restore the conditions for life.

"And, when these conditions are restored, a person will stand tall within themselves and allow the transformation to occur in support of birthing a Christ. It is in the design of our human nature. We are made with the potential to live as Christs, just as our apple trees can produce apples. Your *fruit* may be wisdom, knowledge, faith, healing, miracles, prophesy, discernment of spirits, and speaking in and/or interpreting tongues. But, like the apple tree, these spiritual fruits come when roots run deep, and a person is ready for them.

"When the time is ripe, you will be called to transform your perceptions from the center of the universe being you to resting in the truth that you are one with God, just as a drop of our ocean is one with the ocean. A drop of the ocean may identify itself as separate from the ocean when it splashes about at the tip of a wave, but that is a perception. That same drop has the capacity to identify with the whole of the ocean, knowing that from the ocean it has come and back to the ocean it will return, and never was it not the ocean except within its focus on being separate from it.

"Like that drop of water, you can direct your attention to Christ, to return your attention to what has always been true, that you and your God, the Source of all life, are one and the same. In this transformation of thought, you rest in the desire to shift your life from wanting to <u>have</u> more to realizing you have everything already. You are a Christ just as an apple seed is an apple tree. Now, use it, let that Christ emerge through you."

Laura's tears fell to her neck, carrying dirty remnants from the garden with them. We sat silently as her eyes remained closed and something stirred within her. I touched her hand as she continued experiencing the story, again as if for the first time. After four or five minutes, she broke the silence. "You've never shared this story in that way. It sounded so different than I remember it. What happened to the version you told me before?"

"I'm no longer the person I was, I'm now the person I am, and the story changed as I have changed. What was your experience of it?" I asked.

Her lips quivered as she was unable to get the words out without choking up. But her eyes spoke a thousand lifetimes of words to my heart. We cried as we exchanged love through our eyes in a way I had thought was lost. We were seeing the core of who we each were. The stories we held of our past fell away as images flashed before my inner eyes. Wounds healed that day as God promised. The sins of the world were forgiven. I had heard throughout my life that Jesus saved us from our sins. Now I knew it was true. We are the ones who kept our sins alive. Practicing true forgiveness this day was now magically creating a rich, raw, and very real conversation, allowing God's love to heal *everything*.

REFLECT & CONNECT
Chapters 10 & 11

Before moving forward, pause to reflect on your journey so far.

CH. 10: What is a "red marker" in your life that others might perceive as miraculous, but you've come to take for granted? Reflect on the gifts, abilities, or moments of grace you've experienced.

CH. 11: What is your "seed"? Reflect on your unique gifts or potential that might currently be dormant. What talents, passions, or callings do you feel are waiting to be nurtured and expressed? How can you create the "conditions for life" to allow these to emerge?

DIVE DEEPER - Join the conversation. Explore more thought-provoking questions and share your insights *(including your spiritual gifts) inside* the **O Coalition Portal**.

Scan the QR Code to Enter the Discussion

thelowlyprophet.com/ tlp-reflect&connect

NEXT STEP
Walk the path. Live the transformation.

Continue your Lowly Prophet Transformational Journey with this **engaging discovering process of spiritual gifts**.

Scan to Explore Your Spiritual Gifts

thelowlyprophet.com/tlp-nextstep

TOOL(S) 4: TRANSFORMING:
Gift Assessment

1. Locate TOOL(S) 4 **Gift Assessment** in the Syllabus

2. Watch, Read, and Apply the Resources.

Objective: You will greatly expand awareness and cultivation of your spiritual gifts.

CHAPTER 12
NEW EYES

MEETING LAURA

As we sat together in the garden, I recalled the first time I saw Laura. When our eyes met, time stood still as I saw something I had not known before that moment, like I was oddly remembering our future together. It was more than a premonition. I knew this young woman was the one for me, the one who would become my wife. We had not even known each other's names, but I instantly knew who she was. Despite ignorance of where she had gone to high school or even her hometown, I knew her as I knew myself.

It was like diving into a pool of water and feeling the sensations against the skin knowing I was in a completely new environment. The laws of everything in that water were different from those in the open air. I felt like I belonged in that *water* just as a dolphin belongs in the ocean. I felt alive and wanted more. I wanted to get to know this woman wholly, fully, completely. But what was it? What did I see in those beautiful brown, warm eyes?

The veil between worlds had somehow lifted. I saw Christ in those eyes, I suppose and just… wanted more. After the first date with Laura, my mom came to campus for lunch, and I shared that I'd found the woman I would marry.

"Does she know this, Jack?" My mom asked with a smile and disbelieving tone.

"I don't know. We haven't talked about it. I just know. It's her, Mom."

"How could you know after just one date?" She pressed.

I didn't know how to say that God revealed the truth of my future wife to me before even knowing her name, or that this woman would help me remember my union with God. No, that wouldn't have landed well with Mom. "I can't explain it, Mom. But I know. It's like I've known her my whole life. She's the one."

Laura and I dated for three years before getting engaged. There were times I had my doubts. She didn't always *stop time* for me. In fact, there were situations when she was downright cruel, and I wondered if it was the right thing. But there was something more than the superficial parts of our relationship's ups and downs that kept both of us in it. We were meant for each other and we knew it at a soul level.

We went on to have children and raise a family of four kids, now 12, 14, 17, and 22 years of age. But somewhere along the way I had forgotten who my wife was. I had clothed her with the worldliness of judgments, burdens, hurts, issues, and traumas and lost sight of the Christ I once saw in those eyes. I made a false image of her, one that became my reality.

She was the one who rejected me when I wanted sex. She was the one who gave me a look of disapproval when I wanted to share something meaningful with our kids. She was the one who pointed out my faults and the one I had withdrawn from emotionally. In my mind, she had become something other than who I knew her to be that day we met.

I made a false impression of her, and she knew it. She had done the same to me. I justified it was her fault. *If only she knew how hard I was trying. If only she could see the real me. If only she could love me enough.* But how could she? I clothed myself with false images too, having also lost connection with the truth of who I was.

Laura and I developed patterns that played out automatically. She would complain that I was late for dinner and the kids were misbehaving, and I would rage at the kids for *making* their mom mad and having me come home to *this*! Of course, *this*, had layers of past excuses piled up as a wall between me and their mother.

My anger was misplaced. I didn't know how to begin changing the dynamics. In heated conversations, divorce was mentioned more than once. Laura was both my best friend and worst enemy. I couldn't live with her and was afraid to be without her. We were stuck. The smallest infractions set in motion excuses to depart from each other, retreating to dark corners of our individuality, seeking distractions and temporary pleasures.

An ice cream cone with my son after the big game gave a moment of indulgence that she missed out on while volunteering for the school fundraiser—one point for team Jack. Point after point, we played a game only we knew the rules to. That which started so grand had become a living hell. But God wasn't done with us. While we played footsie with the devil, God was concocting his own plan.

REVELATION

Years before that moment in the garden with Laura, a woman came into my office and asked for help. She was lost in life, and I became known as a spiritual guide and teacher. As I prayed, a mental image appeared of this woman's college-aged son in a difficult situation. He needed intervention.

I said, "listen. You may not have evidence of what is happening with your son but send him a picture of the cast from *Three's Company*, the old TV show from the seventies, and ask him to explain what he's been hiding from you."

She did after our session, and it opened the door to getting him the help he needed.

As it turned out, her son had flunked two courses and hidden it from his parents. Additionally, that semester, he was failing two more classes. Feeling overwhelmed, he withdrew emotionally and was shutting down. A girl in his dorm invited him to church, where he prayed for guidance. Later that day, the *Three's Company* picture arrived from Mom. One of the actors, John Ritter, was the spitting image of his Hall Director. This inspired him to ask the Hall Director for help and he beautifully handled the situation, helping him get support from the school and turn around the situation. At our next session, my client thanked me profusely and asked how I knew to show him a *Three's Company* picture.

"God told me to say that to you," I replied casually. "I don't know much about you, your son, or *Three's Company* that God didn't tell me."

"You're a prophet," she said to me.

I scoffed. "If I were such a prophet, then I would know how to change my relationship at home. I will go home tonight and be dirt on the bottom of my wife's slippers. I am like a roommate, and I am not sure how long she will keep me around."

"I'm so sorry to hear that, Jack, but you might want to redirect your energy to see the good in her. You are so brilliant in casting light into other people's lives. Try doing the same for yourself."

She was right. I needed to be better in my own life. That was well before seeing Jesus, but I spoke to him regularly and thought he could help.

CHANGE

In between clients that day, I prayed, "hey Jesus, what is with the blind spot I have with my wife? Can you help me?"

"Sure," he replied. "You have a few blind spots, by the way. We'll work with your wife if you like, but I propose we start with you. Your blind spot is with yourself. It's easier to project it onto Laura and make her your problem, but if you keep it up, she'll leave, or you'll leave, and your *problem* will be gone, or so you'll tell yourself. You may even find a new love interest after the heartbreak of your marriage dissolving heals up. You may think this new person is so much better than Laura, and quite the love affair for a bit. But eventually, your honeymoon stage will end, and guess who will show up in a new body, with a new name, an interesting career, and characteristics that Laura never had?" Jesus paused to let me digest where he was going.

"Laura?" I asked.

"Yes, Laura," He confirmed. The same issues you have with Laura will show up in every relationship you have and will be especially pronounced at home. So, you can let your marriage dissolve and learn about yourself the hard way, or you can do your best to resolve issues in yourself and have a very real chance of resolving the issues in your marriage."

"I don't know, Jesus. It's gotten pretty bad. Even if I change, it won't mean she will want to stay. I'm willing to try, though." Skeptical but willing, I asked, "where do I begin?"

"The same place you always begin. Take a few nice deep breaths and cancel your goals to make Laura the issue. Allow her to heal in your mind. Let all that you think you know about her dissolve. Let God show you who she is in truth. And then we'll talk."

I started to do this by finding one of my favorite pictures of Laura and setting a reminder daily to look at it and see the highest and best in her. If I judged her, I told myself *that's not her; I collapse this story I made up about her*. This was followed by thinking, saying, and often writing something I cherished about her. Another practice was identifying three things for which I was grateful about Laura on that day. One day, she folded my socks, and another day, she picked the kids up from school. They didn't have to be big things, but feeling gratitude was the point.

Because of this, I started to see more of the Laura I fell in love with. Months into this practice, she criticized me for not cleaning a pan well enough after making eggs, and my old pattern of judging was no longer present. Instead of defending myself, I felt thankful that I married someone so observant and said, "thank you for pointing that out." I cleaned the pan and that was that.

So many things changed. I enjoyed listening to her tell me about her adventure with the neighbor's dog, and I looked forward to making meals together. Our walks became a priority again.

By canceling my goals to be the hero and solve issues, I stopped flying off the handle at our kids if an issue arose between one of them and Laura, encouraging them to engage directly and listen to each other. Most issues worked themselves out without needing me.

I also stopped feeling sorry for myself when she rejected my advances to intimacy. In my case, the truth was I *wanted* to be rejected. It justified my withdrawing from her in favor of doing something I wanted to do anyway: spend time alone, see a movie, go golfing with friends, you name it. If I was justified in my mind, I could leave with no guilt. As my issues around that pattern dissolved, I discussed things directly. "Can I hang out with the guys this weekend?"

"Sure," would inevitably be her reply unless something else was a priority.

Oh, the games we played killed our ability to show up and live life to its fullest. Why would we do that? We were taught how to do this by others who were also out of alignment with their optimal being state, the state of Jesus (the Christ). For a Christ will only teach love and show up in your life as rays of light, bringing you opportunities to live in that same state of Christ. In the world, this person may work as a barber, home-maker, or baker. It could be anyone.

These people may have an invention to make life more delightful. They may manage your finances as a Christ. Christ is alive in the world right now. As it is in Heaven, so it will be on Earth. Soon, it will be impossible to ignore all the Christs in the world. But make no mistake, they may be in this world and look like every other person, but Christ can see the Christ in another, and they support each other, extending love and expressing the good, the holy, and the beautiful from the depths of the Divine into the world.

As my relationship with Laura improved, we fought less. Things that once triggered anger during our darkest times no longer affected me. Issues resolved in me, just as Jesus had suggested, changed the dynamics of our relationship. I no longer wanted to leave. I enjoyed being around my wife and kids again. I learned to love my life.

As I looked into Laura's eyes, her dirty tears streaming down her face, I saw her once again. And without thinking, my lips moved, and I said, "Christ knows you, your name. You have always been known. You know it as well."

She nodded. "Thank you. I needed to hear that. I love you."

And that was the end of an illusion we had made up about each other, that we were outside of God and struggling when, in truth, we had joined as one and were helping each other heal and remember.

REFLECT & CONNECT
Chapters 12

Before moving forward, pause to reflect on your journey so far.

CH. 12: How have you clothed others in false perceptions? Jack realized he had clothed his wife with judgments and false impressions that distorted his view of her. Reflect on ways you might have created false narratives about someone in your life. How might these perceptions be limiting your relationship? Are you willing to let these stories go and see the person in their true light?

CH. 12+: What does it mean to see Christ in others? Jack learned to see Laura with new eyes, recognizing the Christ within her. Reflect on what it would mean to see Christ in others. How can this perspective help you extend love and foster deeper connections in your relationships?

DIVE DEEPER - Join the conversation. Explore more thought-provoking questions and share your insights inside the **O Coalition Portal**.

Scan the QR Code to Enter the Discussion

thelowlyprophet.com/ tlp-reflect&connect

NEXT STEP
Walk the path. Live the transformation.

Experience mental, emotional, and spiritual healing with the Love Exchange.

Scan to Practice the Love Exchange

thelowlyprophet.com/tlp-nextstep

TOOL(S) 4: TRANSFORMING:
Love Exchange Tool

1. Locate TOOL(S) 4 **Love Exchange Tool** in the Syllabus

2. Watch, Read, and Practice using the tool.

Objective: You will heal through the love exchange.

CHAPTER 13
THOMAS

Laura and I decided to go out for dinner to celebrate reconnecting in love, a love much purer and freer than ever before. We arrived at Sullivan's and started with a cocktail and our favorite spicy calamari appetizer. I was floored when she told me an incredible story about her life. Yes, we were married, but on that night, she revealed something new.

When she was a young teen, Jesus came to her. Though a

little old for the toys, she danced about her room with Ken and Barbie. Despite the strangeness of a man suddenly appearing by her dresser, she knew it was Jesus.

"He looked a lot like the Prince of Peace painting—you know that painting from that child prodigy? Oh, what's her name? She was from the Chicago area."

I knew who Laura was referring to, but I looked it up on my phone. Jesus visited Akiane Kramarik when she was just four years old and encouraged her to draw and paint her visions. She painted Prince of Peace when she was eight.

Laura continued her story, sharing that she could nearly see through Jesus when she first noticed him. He told her a story about the dolls girls played with in his day and that he even made a few when he was learning carpentry.

At one point, she lost herself in his eyes and zoned out.

"Laura, when you look in my eyes what do you see?" Jesus asked her.

"I see God," she replied.

"And what do you feel?" He asked.

"I feel I am like you, big, powerful, much bigger than my body feels. I feel happy and bubbles of joy keep rising in me. I would love to feel this way forever." Calm, serene, and lost in the God who loved her, she felt whole, connected, home.

Laura shared how she was never the same after that encounter. A courage missing from her life prior to that moment replaced insecurity. After that, nothing rattled her for she knew what was true, and how this world would never hold any value unless God was in it.

"Laura," Jesus continued, "I want to ask if you will bring a Christ into this world."

"Of course," Laura said. She wanted so much to please Jesus.

"Ok," Jesus said. "When you're 33, you will have a child, and that child will be named Thomas. He is going to change your world. You won't remember our conversation until he is fourteen years old, just as you are today. On the day you remember, your life will begin anew."

Laura looked at me across the dinner table as she paused from sharing her story. "Jack, I just remembered this today as we sat in the grass. I remember! This happened to me."

"Are you kidding me?" I laughed despite being moved to tears. "You played with Barbies at fourteen?" I joked.

"That's the part of the story you want to focus on. How age-appropriate my toys were?" She smiled that cute smile she made when there was a hint of embarrassment creeping through. "Well, if you must know, Jimmy Perkins had just asked me to homecoming, and I was playing out our date with Barbie and Ken. You should have seen Barbie's sequined gown."

We laughed, really having a good time, and I returned to the more important part of the story. "What now? What do we do with Thomas?"

"I don't know," Laura replied. "I do remember something else, though. Jesus said that I would be his *brainchild*."

"What does that mean?" I asked her.

"I think it was his way of telling me that I would have more of an intellectual understanding of God until Thomas woke me up to the alternative."

"I find it hard to believe, Laura, that the boy who has trouble putting a dish in the dishwasher is going to wake anything up for you."

"Well, Jack, we'll have to see. I'm willing to learn from him."

When we arrived home from dinner, Thomas was sitting on

the corner of our living room couch. The light was on and it was late. Everyone else was asleep.

"Mom, Dad, can we talk?"

Laura and I looked at each other, half expecting something like this might occur. Thomas never asked to talk, so this was definitely out of character. "What's up, champ?" I asked, and we sat with him and waited.

"I'm having a hard time with something. I think I like girls," he started, "but I like boys too. And… I'm not sure what to do. I feel confused and quite anxious about it." His hands fidgeted, eyes darted up, down, and all around as he spoke.

Laura sat next to him, put her arm around him, pulled him close, and said, "Thomas, you know we love you no matter who you are attracted to. You'll make the right choice for you."

"Thanks, mom. But that doesn't change the confusion."

"I know, I know. It must feel unnerving feeling confused like that. Is that right?"

"Yes, that's it. Unnerving. I want to feel good about myself, but I don't feel that way right now." Now that Thomas felt supported and heard, he was able to relax. "What do I do?"

"Before we get to that, there are some things you should know about being a teen," Laura answered. "So many hormones and thoughts come into a teen's mind as you navigate growing up, such as being with a girl or a boy. That is normal. Issues tend to surface when those thoughts are suppressed and hidden. The more you suppress, judge, and run from a thought, the more it will chase after you, which becomes unhealthy. We are happy you brought this to us, aren't we Jack?"

"Yes, and your mom is right," I added. "I had thoughts like that too, only I didn't have your maturity, or the guidance needed to deal with it. I did exactly what your mom said not to do. I suppressed my thoughts. I believed something was wrong with me and didn't really deal with it until adulthood, and that was during my mental health crisis. Of course, that was just one thing I suppressed."

Relaxing just a little bit more, Thomas asked, "how did you finally address it?"

"I embraced it, all of it." I wandered off in my mind for a moment as I recalled that period of my life.

"Dad, I want to know. I need to. I'm so confused and need help. There are kids in my class considering hormone pills because they are convinced that they were born the wrong sex. Maybe they were. I wonder about myself sometimes. I feel ashamed of my thoughts. I even…" Thomas's voice trailed off, stopping him from possibly sharing more than he had intended. His eyes fell, and he slunk into the couch like he was trying to hide.

"Thomas," I said, "if you have a thought, I have probably thought it too or done it." To break the ice further, I shared something embarrassing for me that Laura wasn't even fully aware of. At least, I didn't think she was. "When I was thirteen," I continued, "I began exploring my body, just as you have." His eyes darted up, shocked that I would bring up something so personal.

Laura jumped in to help. We were a team again. "Thomas, boys AND girls explore their bodies. It's normal and natural to feel our bodies and understand how they function in all ways, including sexually. Repressing and judging can lead to distorted thoughts, beliefs, and behaviors."

"Exactly," I said. "I repressed the thoughts as much as I could. I felt guilty about touching myself, believing I was bad and that good people were like priests, all without a sex drive. I thought that if I was holy, like a priest, I wouldn't feel excited sexually, especially at *inappropriate* times. I assumed abstinence was easy for a priest. I assumed I didn't have that calling because of how easily aroused I got in high school. I tried to stop the arousal but failed again and again. Shame and guilt grew."

Thomas sat up again and re-engaged in the conversation.

121

I continued. "Then, one day, I put on one of my sister's dresses. I wanted to know what I'd look like as a girl and how it would feel. Did girls feel sexual desires like I did? Did they long for boys like I longed for them? After seeing what I looked like in a dress, I removed it. We didn't have any images of naked girls in our house, and there was no internet, so the closest thing I got to seeing what a girl looked like naked was looking at myself in the mirror with my privates hidden."

"Dad, TMI (too much information), that's weird."

"You nailed it, Thomas. That's exactly what I thought, that no one had ever done that before me. I concluded I was some freak. Being alone was hard for me because thoughts of being weird crept in. Occasionally, even as an adult, I would secretly put on your mom's dresses and *be a woman* for a few minutes. Of course, I knew what a woman looked like, so something else was happening, but what was it? I didn't find out until practicing forgiveness and releasing judgments of myself and others. That's when Jesus helped me understand why I did what I did."

"How so?" Thomas asked. Laura looked interested at this point too.

"He pointed out conflicts in me about worthiness, anger, envy and more. Trying on the dress helped me connect with my feminine qualities, and bring to the surface my judgements, some about my life and others projected upon others, including Adam and Eve, believe it or not. The Holy Spirit helped me unwind some of that, and Jesus taught me how to let judgments go. He helped me let go of my worldview and even how I interpreted events in my life.

"As judgments fell, I felt less and less like a victim and connected more and more with who I was created to be. I shed guilt, shame, hurt, and victimhood. Over time, I learned to love myself and who God made me to be. I stopped trying to be like others and started living more aligned with my talents and interests. I started acting in support of creating the world I wanted to live in. At some point, I lost interest in trying on dresses."

"Are you saying what you did was bad?" Thomas asked, concerned about his own situation.

"No, it was actually unconsciously brilliant for me. Trying on the dresses allowed hidden realities to surface in a gentle way. I learned how judging leads to hiding and restricting. It cuts off access to love. Forgiveness and releasing judgments and pains leads to changes. Whether I ever try on another dress or not is not the point. Healing all distortions separating us from our true nature, love, is the point.

"As I lived more and more in Christ, behaviors of all types transformed to align with love rather than fear or hostility. Since patterns of any type are often generational, the odds are high that my parents had similar issues in their lives. I'm not saying the men in our lineage all tried on dresses, but they likely held ideas, beliefs, perceptions, and judgments that resulted in behaviors that were confusing for them. It's written in the Book of Genesis that things judged, unresolved, and unforgiven will be passed down three and four generations.

"I'm no longer talking about trying on dresses here, Thomas. I'm talking about unresolved pain and distortions passed down through the generations. Studies have shown that the descendants of Holocaust survivors can inherit trauma through epigenetic mechanisms, impacting their mental health and well-being. Children who grow up in dysfunctional or abusive households are more likely to experience similar problems in their own relationships and parenting styles, continuing the cycle. The effects of slavery are another area.

"The odds are high, Thomas, that you inherited unresolved stuff from me, your mom, and our ancestors. That may allow you to surface and heal things that we failed to resolve. Some people live their lives feeling like victims of their ancestry, while others transcend it, heal it, and use the resolved state for good. God can do that healing but it requires willingness from the individual."

"Holy shit," Thomas said, eyes wide, realizing he just swore in front of his parents. "So, you're saying that my life is dictated by my ancestors?"

"Influenced, not dictated. And the sooner you embrace them in love, the quicker you will move through issues in your life. And if you resist, patterns will take root, and the issues will persist. Eventually, I think God plans to have it all cleaned up."

"My issues will persist? It sounds like they're not mine." Thomas, still looking for who to blame for his inner conflicts, seemed to miss my point and looked quite happy that his predicament of confusion wasn't his fault.

I attempted to help him see it again. "Thomas, think about this from Christ's perspective. Christ is the only begotten son of God, yes?"

"I suppose, but you say we are all called to live as Christ."

"Yes," I replied. "All of us will have the opportunity to remain a *caterpillar* or transform into the *butterfly*. The *butterfly*, in this case, is Christ. From that perspective, to become the butterfly, anything blocking the caterpillar from transformation must be removed, cleansed, purified, and made holy. Get it?"

"So, you are saying it doesn't matter that I inherited stuff from my ancestors. I must deal with it if I want to live as a Christ in this world?"

"You get to deal with it," I encouraged him.

"Get to? Get to? Dad, this sucks. I want to know if I'm gay, bi, or cis. I feel alone not knowing. It seems all the other kids know what they are. I feel alone in this."

Reassuring him, I responded, "let's put aside your identity for a moment. Mom and I trust that whatever happens in that department will be right for you. That said, when you shift from *having to* deal with your ancestry to *getting to*, you allow more truth to be seen, and any ideas of victimhood you have will fall away."

"But I am a victim. I didn't do this. Someone else did. You did this," Thomas attacked, clearly feeling scared.

"Perhaps I did but consider a broader view. God created the Christ, the purest form of expression of a human possible. God and Christ are one. The Holy Spirit is the great unwinder of all errors in a person such that they ascend into the Christ, and God brings to Christ everything needed to move deeper and deeper into a relationship with God such that all three persons of that trinity are in sync in a human being.

"That is what Jesus did and taught his followers. He forgave the world's sins and taught us to do the same. Until we do, we are stuck. You are stuck as a descendant of me and your mom, and everyone else on the planet is stuck in their own ancestral muck.

"But you, and you alone, can choose to say yes to clearing out issues that keep you isolated from God. You can accept Jesus as being the truth, the way, and the light. He asked us to live as He lived and promised all of us that if we do that, we, too, will come into union with God. He made it quite clear. All are invited, but few will choose. But you have a choice, and when you choose, you will see that you get to do the work necessary to prepare yourself to live as Christ."

"Why haven't I ever heard this from a priest, Dad? Why isn't my Religious Education teacher saying any of this?"

"They are teaching it," I replied. "If they are teaching you the Bible, you are getting it. It just may be that a filter has been over your eyes, blaming and judging. But it's all there in that Bible you have been learning from since birth."

"Your dad's right," Laura added. "Everything is there, and everything in that Bible is also written perfectly on your heart. Look inside your heart and ask if this is true."

Thomas relaxed and looked from Laura to me and back again before sighing. "I know it's true. What do I do now?"

"Thomas," Laura began, "a Christ-centered person will recognize the goodness in both the divine masculine and divine feminine parts of themselves. So, what you do is explore those parts. The feminine, often associated with intuition, nurturing, emotion, and flow, are strong in our family. The masculine, including strength, action, logic, provision, and protection, are readily available too. Achieving balance between these two is for the benefit of your development and growth. Balancing masculine and feminine energies requires discipline to cultivate both sets of qualities within yourself. In doing so, you will learn to recognize their interplay in different aspects of your life. Prayer, meditation, self-reflection, non-judgment, and gratitude help harmonize these energies. We'll help you with those, but your life path is unique for you."

"Can you give an example of the masculine and feminine in balance?" Thomas asked, appearing intrigued.

"Sure. Give me a second." Laura thought a moment and then lit up. "Ok, I have a few. When balanced, the masculine will take purposeful action toward goals while the feminine aligns those actions with values and wisdom ensuring they're fulfilling on a deeper level. The masculine will maintain physical fitness while the feminine pays attention to mental and emotional health. The masculine speaks with clarity and confidence ensuring an effectively delivered message while the feminine listens actively and empathetically, fostering open dialogue. Exploring your divine feminine and masculine natures is part of the discovery process of living in Christ. Does that help?"

"Yes." He still didn't have his answer but was feeling better about not having it.

"Thomas, if you pray to the Holy Spirit, your path to live in Christ is certain, and I am confident whatever your sexual questions are, they will clear up. Trust that. Though your father and I have different experiences and very different paths, the Holy Spirit knew the path that was right for each of us and the path right for us together in marriage. You can count on it being the same for you."

"Thanks, Mom." He smiled and hugged Laura.

"You'll be ok, sweetie. Be patient with yourself and let go of the idea that all your friends have everything figured out. They don't."

He nodded. "You're right, Mom. They don't." And with that, Thomas got up, hugged me, and headed up to his room.

"Well, that was unexpected," I said to Laura.

"Which part?" Her tone and look indicated she was thinking of me trying on some of her clothes.

"I felt so much shame about it, Laura. I thought I would be devastated if anyone found out."

"I know. I've had my own secret parts, hiding shame, too. Hiding things will do that." She sighed. "Wow, imagine this world when no more shame is left to heal." Laura drifted into her imagination as we sat in silence.

"Thank you, Jesus," I said under my breath.

"You're welcome," came the answer. Jesus had been there the whole time, of course. "Wait till you see what happens next," he added.

His cliffhangers were the best.

CHAPTER 14
THE INVITATION

The next day, Thomas returned from school excited. "Mom, Dad, you won't believe what happened in religion class." He yanked open the refrigerator door and thrust an arm towards the back before pulling out a snack. "Mr. Strazynski told us we're all to become Christs. He went around the room and said, 'Jason the Christ, Marla the Christ, and did this for each of us as he made his point. I thought it was so ironic, considering our conversation yesterday. I told him about you, Dad."

"Excuse me?" I questioned. "Told him what?"

"I said that you had a special relationship with Jesus, that he taught you how to live as a Christ."

"Thomas, I don't know if sharing something like that is such a good idea." I felt my heart race, and my mind jetted to being called in and blamed for corrupting my kids with nonsense. My fears of returning to a mental hospital came in fast. While I breathed and allowed those emotions to move, Thomas continued.

"Dad, it's fine. He loved it. In fact, he wants you to come in and share your story with the class, if you're willing. Dad, they would love it too. You have one of the most fascinating stories ever lived. Please come. Please?"

I sighed. "Alright, I'll do it on one condition. I'll need three hours, and we will do it after school, so it is voluntary. I don't want anyone in the room who doesn't want to be there."

"I'll let him know." And with that, Thomas sent off a text.

Within minutes, Mr. Strazynsky confirmed we would be on in two weeks. This was moving so fast. What would I tell them? How many would show up? When would I have time to prepare? My days were already full. "Lord, I put this in your hands," I whispered. "If you want this and are putting me in front of these students, please show me the way. I trust you."

My phone rang at that very moment. "Hello?"

"Jack, this is Principal Goodwin from Benet Academy. I hear you'll be imparting wisdom to our students on October 3rd. Thank you. I'm just letting you know we'll be in the gymnasium for the occasion, which I'll be announcing to the entire school."

"The entire school? Why is that? I thought this was just for Thomas's class?"

"A few of the faculty have read your books, Jack, and they

want to invite their students too. Is this ok for you?" I had written a few of books about spiritual healing and though they weren't huge sellers, the word had gotten out.

"Uh, yes? Sure. Sure thing, Principal Goodwin. I'm fine with that."

"Great! Then we'll see you on the 3rd at 9 am."

"9 am? I thought we would do this after school, so it is voluntary."

"It will be voluntary, Jack. No one will have to attend. Anyone who chooses not to will have a study hall. Will nine work for you?"

"Ok. Yes. 9 am on the 3rd. I'll need a whiteboard."

"You've got it. We have a digital whiteboard that broadcasts to every student's device making it easy to see whatever you want to share. Thanks for doing this, Jack. We'll see you then."

Suddenly, this was a bigger deal than I had expected. A conversation with Thomas about sexual orientation had turned into so much more. *I'm going to either water down the message or not show up. This is too much.*

"Jack," Jesus broke through my insecurities and doubts. "You don't have to do this, but the Heavens are cheering you on. It is important. Please answer the call. You have been preparing for this since I first knocked on your door. Do you remember?"

"No. I wish I did. Can you remind me?"

"You had prayed for intercession from St. Philomena. You were falling asleep on the couch. I was at your back door with St. Philomena, and we knocked three times. Do you remember now?"

A memory flickered. I had experienced a miracle that day, though I hadn't realized Jesus had been there. "Yes, I remember the knocks," I said slowly. "But I didn't know that was you."

"I'm always with you, Jack, and I'm with you now. Let's get to work. I would like you to visit your favorite coffee shop." An image of Sparrow Coffee in Naperville popped to mind.

"But I have a meeting in 20 minutes," I protested.

"It'll be canceled by the time you get there. Take a notebook and some crayons. Oh, and a pen."

I dropped what I was doing and headed to the coffee shop. On the way, my client called and canceled our appointment. *I love my life,* I said to myself, enjoying the synchronicity of how amazing the world seemed the more in tune I'd become with Christ.

Within hours I had a sketch of the talk and divine instructions on how to effectively reach however many students and faculty turned up. I had an exercise that would show each of them the power of Christ in their lives now and the awe they would experience if they surrendered this life of theirs to God and embraced the transformation awaiting their new life.

Ten minutes before I was to leave for home, a woman approached me. "Are you a priest?" She asked.

"No. No, I'm not. Why do you ask?"

"I can't keep my eyes off you. I've been praying for help and when I looked over, I thought…well… Has anyone ever told you that you have the eyes of Christ?"

In fact, before I was to be married to Laura, an old woman had stopped me at church and asked if I had considered becoming a priest because she also said I had the eyes of Christ. "Yes. I was told that once, a long time ago."

"Do you remember when that was?" She asked.

"It must have been in the early 1990s. I was in Siesta Key at…"

She finished my sentence, "St. Michael the Archangel church?"

"Yes, how did you know?" I asked.

Tears streamed down her face and her legs wobbled as she could no longer hold herself up. Grabbing the table, she sat next to me and sobbed. Upon calming down, she blotted her face with a napkin. "I was ten years old. That day, my grandmother came into the church happier than I'd ever seen her. I asked, 'What's going on, Grandma?' She joyfully replied, 'I think I might meet a friend of Jesus.' I asked her where, and she pointed to a man in his twenties holding the door. It was you. You were that man.'"

I couldn't believe what was happening here. Thirty years earlier, I was indeed at that church holding that door. I remembered it like it was yesterday. "I remember what your grandmother was wearing," I said. "She had a pink and white floral dress. It was one of the most impactful moments of my life."

Now I was crying. This is why Jesus wanted me to come here, or at least one of the reasons.

After exchanging names, she said, "Jack, I prayed today for Jesus to show me he was real. I have felt so lost and was losing hope. My husband died yesterday and left me with three young children. Right now, they're with my sister. I don't know what to do. I need help."

Invite them to the school event, I felt a prompting in my soul. So I did, and Maria agreed to attend, excited at the prospect of feeling better. Neither of us was supposed to be at that coffee shop that morning, yet nothing more perfect could have taken place.

Back home, I asked Jesus if there was anything else for me to know.

"You'll find out soon enough," came the response.

What a day!

That night, I woke up in a sweat. My nerves were getting the best of me. What was I to actually share with these students? My notes from the day flashed before my mind's eye.

Breathe, Jack, I said to myself. *I'm just scared of being exposed. It'll be okay. If Jesus says it will be okay, it will be okay.*

My concern was that even if I were brilliant, my message may be received differently than intended. Jesus's words for his Disciples to dust off their sandals and go to the next town if they were rejected echoed in my mind.

Am I willing to be rejected in my hometown? If this is from God, I'm willing to do it. If not, though, please God, have this go away. Is this the right thing to do?

My whole life, I wondered how Jesus had said 'yes' to being crucified and how saints said 'yes' to martyrdom. Why, in God's name, would they put themselves through any of that? I thought they were crazy, I suppose. Perhaps the irony was that I had gone crazy and was now facing a challenge that felt much harder than healing.

I couldn't back out, even though I wanted to. After decades of inconsistency, my 'yes' had finally become a 'yes'. My life path had become narrower. I had strayed enough over the years to know that straying wouldn't satisfy my soul. Despite saying 'yes', my mind still showed undesirable outcomes as possibilities. Though those fear-induced thoughts rarely seemed to manifest, they still arose under stress. Knowing that acting from fear always produced negative outcomes, I faced it.

Fearful thoughts faced head-on with love always changed those thoughts. And, since experience taught me that knowing the *how* of God's visions was unnecessary, I relaxed into trusting that this talk at Thomas's high school would come together just fine.

While relaxing, I thought of Jesus dying for our sins and rising for our lives. The seed of Christ planted in the fertile soil of Jesus had grown over the centuries, with its branches extending to each of us. I could identify my life as a measly branch at the whim of its vast and powerful *tree*, or I could recognize being whole with the tree, expressing at this moment as one of its branches.

God, I pray that I have the patience to wait for guidance. I surrender and trust.

"Relax." A voice spoke softly through me. "You are ok. I have a message for you. I want you to live a pure, whole, amazing life. We have work to do creating certain projects in the world. *We* includes your brothers and sisters in Christ. *We* includes friends and family members ready to join you. *We* includes *branches* from the Tree of Life who once thought they were separate realizing they are part of the same *tree*. The world is changing. We have one job and one job alone. Allow an opportunity to ripen for all the *branches* to remember they are much more than just a single *branch* going at life alone. We have a duty to wake up the *branches* to what has always been true: They and their *father* are to be reunited as one. The rest will flow from that. Our world is ready. It has been prepared from the moment it was created. It's time. Now, get some rest."

I did rest. The nervousness left. Peace washed over me. God had spoken through me, and never, ever had I felt so close: One with my thoughts, one with my voice, one with me, one with her, one with him. Where God began and where God ended was no longer a question. God was everywhere and in everything. Without God, there is nothing real.

Morning came, and Laura was on the back patio. I joined her. "What's happening?" I asked.

She sipped her morning tea and smiled. "I had the most amazing dream last night," she said. "You were in trouble. A monster was about to get you, and I intervened. I prayed that you be healed in the name of the Father and of the Son and of the Holy Spirit. Amen."

She paused and looked away, recalling her dream. Her eyes were deep and engrossing, radiating unwavering love, once again, reminiscent of the eyes of Christ. I saw it. It's what that woman saw in me at the church so many years ago. That divine essence was visible and touched my soul. It was incredible. Laura returned her gaze to me. "You had a light come out of you and embrace the monster right when I completed the prayer. God then spoke to you and reassured you. He was asking you to help with his projects. He asked me to help, too." I smiled and nodded. "You saw it too, didn't you?" She asked, sensing that I received a visit.

"Not quite the way you experienced it, Laura. But yes, I'm on board. We have work to do."

REFLECT & CONNECT
Chapters 13 & 14

Before moving forward, pause to reflect on your journey so far.

CH. 13: What "secrets" are you holding onto, and how might they be shaping your life? Both Jack and Thomas grappled with feelings of shame and confusion related to hidden parts of themselves. Reflect on any secrets or hidden aspects of your own life. How have they influenced your relationships, decisions, or self-perception? What steps could you take to release these burdens and bring them into God's loving light?

CH. 14: What does it mean to say "yes" to God's call? Jack reflects on his fears and doubts about stepping into a public role to share his spiritual journey. Have you ever felt called to do something outside your comfort zone? What fears arose, and how did you handle them? What would it look like for you to say "yes" to a higher purpose in your own life?

DIVE DEEPER - Join the conversation. Explore more thought-provoking questions and share your insights inside the **O Coalition Portal**.

Scan the QR Code to Enter the Discussion

thelowlyprophet.com/ tlp-reflect&connect

NEXT STEP
Walk the path. Live the transformation.

Accelerate your Transformation now. Disrupt and change unhealthy patterns using the practice of surrender.

Scan to Practice True Surrender

thelowlyprophet.com/tlp-nextstep

TOOL(S) 4: TRANSFORMING:
Surrender

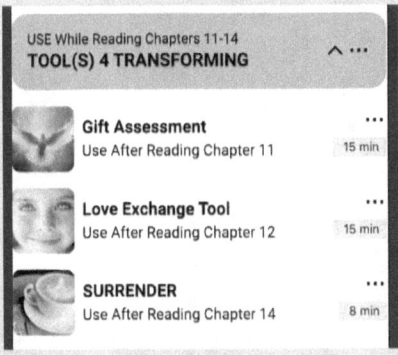

1. Locate TOOL(S) 4 **SURRENDER** in the Syllabus

2. Watch, Read, and Apply the practice.

3. PLUS, Explore **BONUS module: Beatitudes in Action**

Objective: You will practice surrendering (as Jack does in Chapter 14).

CHAPTER 15
THE INTERNET OF GOD

It was the morning of my talk and the gymnasium was standing room only. In addition to students and faculty, a section of the bleachers was secured for a local non-profit focused on mental health. Families gathered who had lost loved ones to suicides and other early deaths. Before the event, the student body president reached out, asking if family members could also attend. All were welcome, and I was ready.

Jimmy Barnes needed consoling after losing his wallet. Mary McMillan needed support in dealing with the pressures of college recruiting. She was a stellar athlete and wanted the right school for her. Abigail Jane ran a red light and reeled from the shame she believed she'd brought upon her parents.

I had a sudden wave of awareness before entering the gymnasium. I didn't always receive names, but I often saw situations and faces. God showed me the various challenging circumstances that Benet Academy's students were facing: Parents out of work, mental health issues, grade disappointments, relationship dramas, faith conflicts, and more. All of this was on display in that gymnasium.

Everyone settled in, and I was introduced. Standing quietly for a moment, I scanned the crowd and surrendered. "In preparation for today," I began, "God revealed the message I'd be sharing. Before I do, there's somewhat of a big secret you should know. Though I have received a preview of God's message in my spirit, I have no awareness consciously of exactly what I will share with you today. God sends His word to me in *streaming downloads*, much like you receive a movie on your phone. Just because you load up the show doesn't mean you know its contents, right?

"However, just like with movies, these downloads always comes with a preview. I receive what is relevant to the person or group I'll be working with so that I am prepared to be as pure a vessel possible for God's message. I trust God knows what is optimal to share. This may sound strange if you have never had an experience like this, but God has trained me for years to trust breath by breath, word by word, sentence by sentence.

"Whether you are aware of them yet, you all have unique gifts just like this one. In this regard, think of your mind-body system as a way more advanced version of your phone. When properly tuned, some pretty remarkable features get activated.

"Like you, I have my history, content, *tools*, and *apps* that reside on my *device's hard drive*, but for moments like this, I surrender my ways to God. Like an apple tree might be in awe of its first apple, I was in awe as God revealed this tuning process which supported healing from a mental health crisis.

"I will share that story with you, the dark night of my soul, and the illumination of love that changed me from a *desktop computer with no internet access* to the latest and greatest model with instant *streaming resources*. Would you like to know how to unwind all obstacles in your life and tune in to the only true source of love, which will transform your life into what is possible for you? Would you like that? If so, you are in the right place."

I took a moment to scan the faces. People nodded. Many leaned in.

"Our seventeen-year-old daughter, Josephine Shay (aka, Shay), raised two fists showing support. The principal took a cell phone away from a disengaged senior and held it up for others to see, sending the message to show up. A few late arrivals opened the gymnasium doors to enter quietly, but a squeaky hinge exposed them. Silence hung in the air for just a bit. Feeling an inner prompt, I continued.

"Now, some of you may doubt what I am saying. Some may question my sanity for even proposing what I said already. Some may now want this more than ever. And some may never want it. Whatever you are thinking, I ask that you suspend any conclusions. Allow yourself to listen from your heart and free this experience from judging or seeking ways to make what I say right or wrong. Let your ideas about Jesus expand and see him with new eyes. Let yourself experience God's love in new ways. Are you ready for this?"

A gentle applause ensued while a woman walked from the back wall to the gymnasium floor. It was Maria from the coffee shop. Her children stayed behind as she approached me and reached for the microphone.

Though unexpected, I let her speak, and the crowd hushed as she began. "If you desire to know the power of Christ, you must listen to this man. The day after my husband of ten years died, I was questioning whether Jesus was real." She told the story (through a few emotional pauses) of seeing me at ten years old, standing in the doorway of St. Michael the Archangel church in Sarasota. But she added something. "What Jack doesn't know," she said, "is that I wasn't going to come here today, even though I said I would.

"That is until a man appeared in my bedroom this morning and woke me up. It was Jesus himself. Nothing like this has ever happened to me. He knelt by my side and held my hand, and a scene appeared in my mind. In that scene, I was standing before you all, sharing this story. He showed me how important it was to be here today. He pointed out a girl in the front row wearing a red blouse."

Maria walked toward a girl in the front row wearing a red blouse and softened her tone. "He told me you have been tormented in your mind about something that happened when you were four years old. He showed me what it was and that your mom died shortly after. You thought it was your fault and couldn't stand yourself. This judgment you hold onto is fueling suicidal thoughts. If you let Jesus show you the truth, those thoughts will stop. Grab my hand and let him show you."

Initially uncomfortable being called out in front of the school, the young girl gave in to the moment, oblivious to her friends and schoolmates. She stood and reached for Maria's hands. In an instant, Jesus appeared to the girl along with the spirit of her mother. Her mom pointed to a video screen that only this girl could see, which played a *movie* about how her mother actually died.

Her death had nothing to do with the daughter, and the blame this young girl placed upon herself shattered into a million pieces. The girl fell to the ground, praying. Tears streaming down her face, she was surrounded quickly by friends hugging her and helping her to her feet. "Thank you," she said to Maria before retaking her seat.

Maria returned the microphone to me, whispering, "you've got this," and squeezed my hand as the applause erupted.

I didn't need to respond, just remember:

That morning was extraordinary. The exercises were perfect in helping people realize the Christ within themselves, not just intellectually, but as an experience. I drew caterpillars. I talked about prophets and seeds. I asked the students to consider who they were. Exercise after exercise, students and faculty began to experience the Christ within themselves. The gentle buzz of the crowd that began the event evolved into a harmonious hum of spirit and energy.

Interested in trying the exercises yourself? Get started with this brief masterclass:
thelowlyprophet.com/masterclass

After the event, dozens gathered around me to share their appreciation and experiences, including several miracles that morning. But one person wasn't happy at all and called me a fraud.

Seething with anger, he stayed back until the gym was nearly empty. I could have sworn he was foaming at the mouth, but that might be an exaggeration. He wanted to know where I had gotten this blasphemous rhetoric and how dare I teach it to children. He called the girl in the front row a plant and the interruption from Maria a staged event. He couldn't stand me.

Noticing my desire to be liked surfacing, I quickly canceled my goals for him to understand, for him to have compassion, for him to accept me and be anything other than who he was at that moment. I released trying to control the situation, let egoic needs fall away and found, amidst his yelling, peace, and calm. *Embrace him in your love,* and I prayed silently for God's love to show up.

I felt a shift in me as obvious as a light being turned on in a dark room. Suddenly, he fell silent as his eyes moved away from me, fixated on something over my shoulder. I looked and saw nothing, and an expression of confusion emerged on his face before re-engaging.

"I'm sorry," he said, "what was I saying?" *Could he have forgotten already?* He was so passionate.

"You were telling me how full of crap I am, I believe. Would you like to continue?"

He stammered, rocking back and forth. "Um, um, well." Then, looking away again and pointing over my shoulder, he asked, "do you see that? It's an angel."

I couldn't see what he saw and told him, "I don't. It's for you to see, I suppose. I do believe you, though."

"Uh, I guess I'll go now. By the way, my name's Jelejia." He reached out and shook my hand. "I work in the computer department here. I did like your analogy in the beginning. Is it true what you said?" He asked sincerely.

"Yes. As far as I know, all of it is true," I replied.

"Well, thank you then. You had a tough go of it for a while. I'm glad you made it through. Do you really believe this will help people heal their mental illnesses? By coming to Christ?"

"As I said, I think the core reason for all mental illnesses, other than physical injuries or birth dynamics, is the separation of our species from the truth that God is calling us into unity, reunion, and reconciliation. He wants us whole again, and our resistance keeps that from happening. Resolve that, and I think we will all experience more sanity in our lives and worldwide. The body still needs support correcting itself in the physical world, but I believe our best path is revealed when our spirit is right."

"Perhaps you're right. My apologies for my anger. My parents were manipulated by someone who claimed to be a prophet. It led to their divorce, and I never forgave him for doing it, or my parents for their naivety. Had I not seen that angel, I would have left here believing you were just like the other one. He convinced them a catastrophe was coming, and they gave money to build a shelter for church members. He took the money but, as far as I know, he never built anything."

"Well, I don't tell fortunes or claim to know anything about our future. As far as God has informed me, he uses people where they are, but we are human. We have flaws. In the Bible, even Peter could walk on water as his eyes were set on Christ. But what happened when he turned his eyes toward the storm?"

"He sank," Jelejia answered.

"Right. This is no different. I happen to believe we have the potential to live in Christ one hundred percent of the time. I don't claim it to be true for me or anyone I know. But I believe it is possible because God says it's possible. However, it takes a commitment to surrender any perceptions or beliefs blocking that. It takes a willingness to let our wounds surface, release trapped emotions from our past, and let God's love embrace and heal them. It takes discipline to practice the Beatitudes and live the Lord's prayer. It takes courage to admit we, our parents, and others may have been wrong. You know the promise that as we forgive, we are forgiven. Well, maybe it is time to release the pain you have been holding onto about your parents and this prophet you once met."

"You're right," he sighed. "Maybe I was wrong. Maybe I'm not even remembering the circumstances accurately. I need to forgive my parents. I must allow God into this pain and forgive them." It was a start, and a grand start at that. A large, involuntary breath moved through him, and a look of sadness crossed his face. His body shuddered, followed by another deep breath. Soon after, a smile returned, and his eyes widened.

"There you go," I said, acknowledging whatever shift just happened. "That's a start. Now, don't be surprised if..."

Jelejia's phone interrupted me, and he looked to see who it was. "Oh, my gosh. It's my dad. I haven't spoken with him in like twenty years."

"Go ahead and answer it. Sometimes, this is how forgiveness works. The energy of healing can be felt across time and space. Trust me, his call is no coincidence. I guarantee that."

Jelejia said thank you before turning to answer the phone. I knew it was common that releasing emotionally charged issues can lead to the universe reflecting the change, but that phone call came quickly. Once again, I saw how love can move *mountains* that once appeared as impossible obstacles. That one crumbled fast.

Speaking of crumbling fast, this idea of being a prophet was stressful. I returned home and asked Jesus to help restore what is true in my heart.

"Jack, I will tell you what is happening. It is normal for you to go into reaction when you are uncomfortable. You worry about living as a Christ, don't you?"

"Yes, of course. What if I fail? I'm starting to feel the pressure."

"Well, you were on target this morning at the school. You raised enough questions in the right people to make a difference.

They will need nourishment, and I will bring it to them. You've done well. And relax, allow yourself to screw up."

I objected. "But you're perfect. I want to be like you."

"Jack, in the *frequency of Christ*, you experience perfection too. We are all perfect in that union. You are still learning, though. Plan on failures. Learn from them. Doesn't a child fail to walk her first time? The child lets go of the couch to take those first steps and then plops back to the ground. Do you see the success of the first steps or the failure of falling down? Like that child, you will grow. Strength, wisdom, courage, trust... Be the love you were created as, and the rest will follow." He made it sound so easy, which only raised my insecurities.

Looking for reassurance that I was doing it right, I asked, "how do I do that?"

Jesus obliged. "You wake up in the morning and ask to experience the perfect love of Christ. Ask, 'What would it take to be who God knows is available for my life?' Ask, 'What is optimal for today?' And trust the answers. What you ask for in prayer will be given to you. Release (forgive) anything in the way of those prayers being answered. Now, we begin."

And with that, I was alone. I was alone in this idea. *Do I want this, really? Am I willing to go through the challenges necessary to have a relationship with Christ constantly? Am I alone in this?*

"No," came an answer from within. "I am the Holy Spirit, and I'll do everything to support this happening."

"Why?" I asked, still looking for validation that I was ok.

"Be who you are and celebrate that your life is a beacon for others to see their own potential. Now, let's address some situations. Living as a Christ, you must unwind your patterns of deception. You're still seeking approval from others that you are kind and holy. You *are* kind and holy. Let people have their perceptions. God desires to dwell within each of them, too. They may never see you how you are. It won't matter. Keep your eyes on God. Trust the rest."

"Easy for you to say. It's not your life," I said, hearing my snarky tone.

"Right, I suppose you think I'm somewhere on a mountain in the sky broadcasting from a secluded tower with angels brushing my hair and feeding me fine foods, that I am immune to what you experience? Well, let's set the record straight. I am whole in you, and I know everything about you and feel everything you feel. Once you asked for help, you got it. Grab a pen," God's Holy Spirit guided.

Pen in hand, I opened my journal. Having done this dozens of times, I took a few breaths. My hand soon lifted, and God, as one with me at that moment, began to write:

"I am the one you call God and have always been with you. I am who you are. You moved your attention from me for a time, making other people's opinions more important. That was *God* for a while. Now, you can keep that *god* or let it go, as you have other *gods* over the years. The one true God is Love, is Jesus, is you at your core, and that is only revealed in Christ.

Now, don't let your ego run wild. You are, indeed, a part of the totality of God, which is vast beyond human comprehension. On your part, though, you can live in Christ, in the wholeness of God. You can understand why Rumi said, 'You are what you seek'.

You have found and simultaneously been found. You have knocked, and the door has opened. You are alive for the first time and have always lived. You were there at the beginning, at the end, always. The God who is all things real is here now and always will be.

You can choose to focus on God and be part of this wholeness, or leave for the *greener pastures* of the world. Jesus showed you and all the world that there are no greener pastures, and in me is the only life possible. Anyone who wants to look elsewhere can do so, but what is true has always been true. There is only God."

Putting the pen down, I asked, "but why do this at all? Why have an earth, humans, and other life forms across your creations?"

"Our creations," the Holy Spirit shared. "These are our creations. We are in this together. Without me, you are nothing, and without you, I have only my imagination with no manifestation. I love extending the good, holy, and beautiful into manifestation; you get the free will to experience it as you do. I invite you to experience it in complete surrender, entirely one with my Love.

"The prodigal son came home for a reason, and many are coming home today. It will continue getting harder to live in this world apart from me. It is lonely, empty, and frightening to do so. If you remove me from your life and society, the world will reflect that change, becoming more chaotic and unfulfilling. The less I am part of this world, the more insane it will appear. The equivalent is a child running alone in the desert—undesirable by any measure.

"After my children *wander the desert,* failing to find what they seek, leaders will emerge to guide them home to the promised land. Jack, people are dying in the *desert*, yet the solution is in front of their faces. Those who ask for help are given the eyes to see and find it. Those who have found it are called to help others. You answered that call. Now help."

"How?" I asked.

"You'll see. It is time to go now and water your flowers. They are thirsty. Ask them if they know me."

REFLECT & CONNECT
Chapters 15

Before moving forward, pause to reflect on your journey so far.

CH. 15: What does it mean to trust in divine guidance?
Jack demonstrates profound trust in God by stepping into an unknown and daunting situation. Have you ever faced a moment where you felt called to act without knowing all the answers? How did trusting (or not trusting) influence the outcome?

CH. 15+: What obstacles block your connection to love and truth? The Holy Spirit helps Jack identify patterns of seeking approval and deception as barriers to living fully in Christ. What patterns, beliefs, or habits might be limiting your ability to live a life rooted in love and authenticity? How can you begin to address and release them?

DIVE DEEPER - Join the conversation. Explore more thought-provoking questions and share your insights (*including using the Beatitudes*) inside the **O Coalition Portal**.

Scan the QR Code to Enter the Discussion

thelowlyprophet.com/ tlp-reflect&connect

NEXT STEP
Walk the path. Live the transformation.

In this Masterclass, you will practice the exercises from Chapter 15: connect with your true self, ease your mind, release blocks, and align with your highest potential.

Scan to Engage in the Masterclass

thelowlyprophet.com/tlp-nextstep

TOOL(S) 5: Masterclass

1. Locate TOOL(S) 5 MASTERCLASS in the Syllabus

2. Watch, Listen, Read, and Apply the Practices

Objective (Masterclass): Apply the Beatitudes—core teachings of The Lowly Prophet—to bring deeper transformation and spiritual alignment into your life.

Objective (New Eyes): You will be curious and interested with "new eyes" and "new ears"

CHAPTER 16
THE COLOR "YES"

Arriving in our garden, I unwound the hose to water the flowers. They definitely needed it as the vibrant colors had bent and drooped a day or two longer than normal. God asked me to speak to them, so I did. "Hey, flowers, are you thirsty?"

"Oh yeah," came an answer. "Thank you."

It didn't surprise me to hear them *speak* to me. The first time it happened I was confused as I didn't think other things in creation could speak or had been conscious. I learned how wrong I was when a leaf scolded me for calling it a leaf.

"If you focus on my being a leaf," it began, "you miss the fullness of my expression as a tree. I am one with the tree."

That conversation opened my mind to possibilities beyond what I had considered. I guess it was one of the first times I thought it was true that we are one with God. I was like the *leaf* on a tree identifying myself as separate, rather than one with God. I was seeing God in everything, including the flowers.

After watering and seeing the thirsty flowers soak it up and glisten in the sunlight, I asked, "I know this sounds strange asking a flower this question, but do you know God?"

"Of course," came the answer. The flowers answered as one voice to me. "Our creator planted us in a garden and nourished us into life."

"That's not what I meant," I suggested. "I know a gardener planted you at some point, but you were a seed before being planted. Where did you come from?"

"Our lineage returns to the first seed, just as yours does."

"But where did the first seed come from?"

"Our mind," came the answer.

"Our mind?" I asked for the flowers to explain.

"Yes, we all came from the one Mind that created everything. We were created in the image of that Mind that knew what it wanted and manifested us, and continues to manifest. You were held in that Mind as an image and here you are."

"But how?" I asked. "How is that possible?"

"Have you ever been hungry and imagined a meal?"

"Yes," I said.

"You created the meal in that image, yes?"

"Ok, I get that, but I have hands, and everything needed to create that meal."

"And you don't think our creator has hands?" The flowers responded.

"You're saying our creator has giant hands?" I asked.

"No, not in your form. It has everything it needs to create whatever it wants, just as you did for your meal. You don't have a total understanding of God. You only know the aspect you need to know for this life. As flowers, we know the experience of being a flower, and how to interact with our environment for the best life possible as a flower. We bring beauty and joy to people. We are food for insects and animals. We help perpetuate life. We even give back to the earth when our life ends. We help our creator by putting everything into being who we are. We suggest you do the same."

The flowers had a point. If I was going to be fully who I could become, I needed to stop fretting about why I was here and start asking *what* I could do *while* I was here.

What is my purpose? I asked myself. "To live as the best Jack I can," came an answer from within at the same frequency as God's voice, the Christ alive in me.

How do I do that?

"Let go of trying to be special. Let go of resisting your ability to hear God's voice. Let your fear of feeling like an outcast be felt. Let it all come to the surface, and let God inform you."

How?

"It's your trial. You can judge yourself as never being good enough or let the truth be known about you. God chose you to send a message to this world. He chose you amongst all people at this time to share a story that needs to be told."

And now, we begin.

The sun rose to midday, and the flowers were breathtaking, but no flower has ever known how hard it is to be a human.

"Yes, we do," came a response to my thought. "We know, but we don't have that experience. There's a difference."

"How so?" I asked.

"How did you know we needed water?" They asked.

"It came to my attention in a conversation I was having with…" And it struck me who I was having the conversation with. I had identified God as a human person in magnificent form. Perhaps I was wrong. God is so beyond my understanding. Here, a flower was teaching me about my existence. How did it know?

"I'll tell you how we know," came the response. "We are all connected by the same essence that created everything. You shifted your awareness from the apparent separate part of the wholeness of God known as Jack to a higher frequency of love. In that frequency, you were informed that another part of the wholeness of God, us flowers, needed something. Our need for water was brought to your attention, and you chose to water us. Thank you."

They continued. "That is how it always works. In your grocery store, you meet a person feeling sad and think of buying them a flower. They perk up just as we perked up with the water. Had you chosen not to buy them a flower, perhaps the next person in the store would have. But you said 'yes'. We are all one, and we support each other when we say 'yes'. But it is still everyone's free will to do so.

"Whether red or yellow, a flower can bring joy to people. Many people have a *color*. Yours has always been *'yes'* and always will be. You say 'yes' when called upon for your family, a friend, a neighbor, a corporate titan, or the person on the street. Heck, you even said 'yes' to us thirsty flowers. When you say 'yes' to Christ, you say 'yes' to every life form possible living in harmony as a creation in God's Kingdom, and that Kingdom stretches well beyond the *walls* of the *castle* we know as Earth."

The flowers were right. I was saying 'yes', a very big 'yes' to everything except that purpose God laid on my heart. It was time to release putting myself down as less than capable and say 'yes' to sharing a healing message. Even with my 'yes', I assumed a miracle was needed. It wouldn't be the first time.

CHAPTER 17
ROOKHA D'KOODSHA

Our high school senior, Shay, sent a note to Laura and me for a project aimed at shifting high schoolers' focus to gratitude and appreciation, which was perfect for her salty personality. She was a whirlwind of a girl, playing everything like it was a sport. This, of course, came with occasional injuries.

One night, around the age of four, Shay punctured her ear drum after leaving Q-tips in her ears as she prepared for bed. Her quarterback brother had tossed a toothpaste bottle in the air and she'd jumped to receive the pass, lost her balance, and hit the wall, Q-tip first. You may be cringing right now, so I'll spare you the rest of the details, but her eardrum was punctured. Her screams that night were awful, and since the doctor said nothing could be done until morning, we comforted Shay until she settled down and fell asleep. Laura and I explored the internet for everything about ears and how to proceed.

Despite the help of the best doctor in town, there was only a slim chance, just five percent (due to the large-sized hole), that the simplest surgery would fully support the repair. The alternative surgery involved a skin graft taken from behind her ear to create an alternative eardrum. We chose the five percent solution, which entailed cauterizing (burning) the area around the hole and placing a special medical paper over it. The cauterized skin then grows toward the middle of the hole, guided by the paper. Ideally, the hole would close completely, repairing the eardrum with fully restored hearing.

With the odds of success so low, we prayed with Shay for a miracle. After the surgery and months of visiting the doctor, he said, "I don't get it. The hole is healing nicely, but the skin should have stopped growing toward the hole's center long ago. I've never seen anything like this. Let's give it a bit longer. It may just work."

The eardrum eventually healed completely, and our family experienced our first miracle together. It was incredible. The joy we had about receiving such a gift can't be expressed in words.

This belief in miracles was reinforced over the years and led to my praying for a miracle for myself when Marcus and I met at that behavioral health facility. You may recall that after Jesus visited him in his dream, Marcus pointed out that I was denying my prophetic nature. He was right, and I prayed to find my way past that denial and someday repay Marcus if I did.

Like Shay, it seemed that my miracle prayer was being

answered. The training with Mary Jo and everything since then opened a fearlessness in me. Life's *coincidences* compounded. I saw prophecy as a gift from God and felt a responsibility to honor it and honor God by sharing the Divine messages. It was now time to thank Marcus, but I was unable to connect with him as I didn't even know his last name. I asked God if there was anything I could do for Marcus to follow through on my promise.

"Yes," the answer came. I had learned to know God's voice, just as I knew Laura's or anyone's voice with whom I was in a relationship. It showed up in various forms, but it always came in love. Welcoming a friend at our front door is like knowing anyone who came in God's name. It might be Mary, mother of Jesus coming with a guiding message. It could be Jesus or any number of Prophets or Saints. They all vibrate in a frequency range of expansiveness and glory to God. They live. Perception plays a big role here too. As a Christian, I have a framework of words that match Christian stories. If I were Hindu, I would have Hindu stories, and if I were Muslim, I would have Muslim stories. However, the truth of where God is and how to restore our lives to be one in his love is universal. Words get in the way sometimes. The frequency of love, though, is everywhere. God is everywhere. And we get to live purely in that holy state that Jesus lived in and that I know of as Christ.

Back to my promise to God about Marcus, I responded to His "yes" with, "please lead the way."

"I will, but first, let's prepare." I felt my body adjust and move into a position of relaxation. An energy flowed up through me. My body moved, but it was this active force of God doing the moving. Imagine seeing your hand lift off the ground, but you weren't lifting it. It may sound freaky, but it wasn't at all.

I was gently moved into a lotus sitting position, and the image of a home appeared in my mind, a run-down ranch, light blue with white shutters. A blue and red gnome was in the front yard near a water well pipe, sticking out two feet from the grass.

At the end of the gravel driveway was a rusted mailbox with the number 7843. An image of a honeysuckle bush flashed before my eyes with the word *Lane* written across the bush in white text. I knew of a Honeysuckle Lane in our area. A calendar with *Friday* and *2 pm* circled then flashed before my mind's eye. I asked if there was anything else, and the answer came, "Yes, you will be prepared before attending. Be vigilant in your awareness and trust the Mind of God."

I then heard, "it's time. Let's go." I stood, walked to the computer, and mapped the house. A street view showed the light blue ranch God had revealed moments earlier.

As far as I could tell, this had three moments of preparation. First, I received three emails about how people who struggled before learning about Christ's teachings were massively changing their lives and health. This was unusual, as I had never received three emails like that, and their messages all closed with, "In God we Trust. Keep doing what you are doing!" None of the three knew each other, so the odds of all three sending a message and closing in the exact same way was my sign that this could be a God thing.

The second moment of preparation: My wife told me I should help a friend of hers whose son was anxious and violent. When I reminded her that I was not a counselor, she told me that I knew more about mental illnesses than every counselor she had come across. I then reminded her that she didn't know any counselors, and she smiled. "What are you so afraid of? You can help these people. You don't need to heal them since you can't heal anybody anyway. Just help them remember what you remembered, that they are one with God's perfect love, and anything in the way of that must go. You know how to do that. What more do you need? God will do the rest. The counselors and doctors have their roles. Let them do their jobs, but how many are helping with this piece? Trust God and give yourself a holy break. You've got this."

Laura's encouragement touched a spot in my heart that I hid about fearing failure. That fear left me suffering in silence, watching but not interfering with others' struggles. Deep down, I think I wanted to suffer to *get God's love.* I thought suffering would bring me closer to God. Perhaps I rejected my mission to stay in that state of suffering. After Laura opened my mind to this, I took a walk along a local nature trail near the DuPage River.

The third moment of preparation happened on that walk where there was a little girl of about four sitting all by herself under some trees, crying. Glancing around for her parents, I asked, "are you okay?"

Between sobs, she said, "no," and shook her head. It was getting late, and the sun was disappearing over the horizon.

"Is your mom or dad around?" I asked.

"No. I ran away from them."

"Why?" I noticed her look up to the tree and followed her eyes to where a balloon had gotten stuck. "Were you chasing after your balloon?" I asked.

"Uh-huh," she nodded.

Just then, a gentleman of about forty years of age came running from around the bend. "Sara!" he exclaimed, thrilled to find that the girl was safe. "Oh, honey, we didn't know you ran off. Did you lose your balloon?" She pointed up, and he quickly climbed the tree and grabbed it for her.

"My name is Jack," I told him as he landed on his feet holding a yellow balloon.

"Oh, sorry. I should have said hello. I'm Father Jones. This is my niece, Sara. We were having a picnic near the water and lost sight of her for a minute. That was quite a scare. Her parents are out of town, and she and her two younger siblings are with me." He saw my concern about the other two as I looked toward the bend. "Oh, don't worry, a neighbor of theirs is with the other two. She's helping me keep an eye on them. We'll need to do

160

better. Thanks for stopping for our damsel in distress. Balloon crisis averted."

"Father, can I ask you a question?" I posed, noticing the convenience of a pastor being nearby.

"Sure thing." We walked and talked as Sara ran back to her picnic.

"I was wondering, Father, what is your opinion about us living as Christs? I mean, what I've experienced with the Holy Spirit's guidance is an unwinding of issues and patterns in my life. I feel more and more in-tuned to living as Christ. Do you share that?"

"Sure. The more we live free of sin, the closer we become to God. Jesus gave us a model and the gift of the Holy Spirit to help. We are all called to live like Christ." He paused and looked at me. "You think you are there, don't you?"

"I don't know. I have had such a contrast of separation, and now God has revealed himself in so many ways. I see God more and more frequently. He seems to be everywhere."

"Yes, but can you see God in the murderer?" He asked. "Can you see him in the crooked politician? Can you see him in the negligent guardian?" He laughed as he pointed out his own negligence with Sara.

"No. I can't say that I see God in a murderer. I still get quite upset at the crooked politicians, too." Despite his gross examples, his point was made. I still judged.

"It's ok to feel upset," he said, "it's even ok to see evildoers and take action to address evil. However, I think Jesus the Christ, only saw with the eyes of God. In that case, he must have seen the murderer as a lost soul who needed guidance, love, and correction—to be invited to return to right action.

"Whether the murderer chooses to walk that path is another story. That is free will. I wouldn't want the murderer to be watching over my kids, but I might if I knew he had been truly redeemed in Christ. And, like God, I would want evidence of trust in small matters with that person before trusting in large matters."

"That makes sense," I pondered.

"Then it will make sense to you that you are being trusted in larger matters. That means you have passed many tests, but you're not done. There is no finish line, Jack. God is providing you a mission to share the Gospel with people in a way that supports their well-being. Along the way, you will change too. You will expand and grow in your understanding and relationship with God."

"How do you know that?" I asked him.

"Well, I too am a prophet," Father Jones surprised me, then continued. "I have been given much in terms of knowing God's will for people. He shares life paths with me and asks me to reveal insights for people who need a bit of a nudge. You are like the bird that flutters off the ground but not too far without looking down and landing again as the nerves impact your ability to fly. I say unto you, your wings are meant to be used. Use them. Help the people God brings into your life. Give them hope. Give them tools. Help them know their true path to freedom that always comes with God's love."

"Thank you, Father. Thank you." We shook hands, and I waved to Sara and the others sitting on the blanket.

"Thank you, mister," Sara grinned, balloon in tow.

"You're welcome," I replied.

"Oh, one more thing, Jack," the priest called to me. "The depth of Christ is vaster than the ocean, so you will always have more to explore, more to embrace, more opportunities to expand the good, the holy and God's beauty wherever you find yourself. Stay open to learn as much as you teach."

With that we said our goodbyes and I was on my way.

As Friday approached, I freed up my afternoon for 2 pm and beyond. While driving out to Honeysuckle Lane, I marveled at how God's love guided me throughout the week. Perfection. Perfection. Perfection. Nerves fluttered in my belly as I arrived at the light blue ranch. I pulled over before the driveway and took a few breaths to relax. *God, I give this over to you. Walk before me into that house, and may your will be done. Amen.* I always prayed before meeting people. *Is there anything for me to be aware of, Lord?* I asked.

"Be present. Allow God's love to go into this man. It's time."

Walking up the drive, I heard a lawn mower in the backyard. The one-acre lot was in mediocre condition. A few plants and bushes decorated the front, and virtually no landscaping was wrapped around the sides or back. The lawn had bare spots every twenty feet or so.

A rider mower trundled around the yard with dust and grass clippings shooting out its deck. An older gentleman was at the wheel and remained unaware of my presence. I continued towards the back patio and glanced across the yard, watching the mower. Finally, the man looked up, surprised to see me standing there.

He drove up and asked, "who are you?" as he parked and turned off the mower's engine.

"My name's Jack. I was sent here from God." Just kidding. I knew better than to open with a line like that. Instead, I said, "my name is Jack. I'm not sure quite why I'm here. Can you tell me your name?"

"Roger. I'm Roger." And as he told me his name, I saw an image of Marcus from the hospital.

Trusting this, I asked, "is there a Marcus who lives here?"

"Why do you ask?" He questioned, slightly furrowing his brow.

Deducing from his question that he knew Marcus, I said, "we

met a while back, and I wanted to give him a gift. Does he live here?"

"Yes. He does. Let me get him."

Roger stepped through the sliding back door and yelled for Marcus to come meet a visitor. Stomping feet resounded through the house and, soon enough, Marcus appeared at the door.

"Oh my gosh, you came. I don't believe it. You heard my call. You showed up and right on time. Thank you. Oh my God. You're ready, aren't you? You are ready, my friend."

Roger and I exchanged glances. "That's Marcus for you," he said, apologizing with his eyes for Marcus's unusual behavior. "Always up to something. I'll let you two get after it." Roger returned to the mower as Marcus and I embraced.

"It's loud outside," he said, gesturing for me to enter after him.

I followed him to the kitchen table where we sat. "How did you know I'd be here?" I asked.

"I've been asking God to send you every week, but only to let you have the message when you were ready."

"Ready for what?" I asked him.

"You don't know? I asked God how I would heal from my mental illness, and your face came to mind, but I knew you weren't ready since we had just been in the hospital together. You still had to find your teacher and do whatever you have done along the way. So, I asked God to please send you on a Friday at 2 pm, but only when you were ready. And here you are."

"Why Friday at 2 pm?" I asked.

"It's the time before Jesus died on the cross. I knew this work would entail a death and rebirth. I wanted to honor Jesus and his loving sacrifice to leave this world and open the gift of the Holy Spirit for the benefit of all of us. He is the great savior of the world. I am ready when you are. Let's get on with it. How do we start?"

This was a lot to take in. I excused myself for the bathroom, thinking of the image Father Jones gave me of a bird in flight, wondering if I would move above the fear and soar or crash back to the security of land. Laura's encouragement and the memory of those emails closing with "In God we trust" all came rushing forward. I washed my hands and stared in the mirror where a painting in the reflection caught my attention. It was a little girl on her father's shoulders, reaching up to pull a yellow balloon out from a tree. *"Ok, God, I get it. You want me here. Well, I don't know how to even begin. You'll have to show me. Be here now, God. Amen."*

Returning to the kitchen table, I sat down and asked if we could pray together. Marcus agreed, and we continued, inviting God's Holy Spirit to guide our conversation.

These prayers all unfold uniquely but share common elements. Despite being counter-intuitive, we began by letting go of expectations. We then canceled any goals for healing to happen as we thought it should or could. This opened some emotion in Marcus, and I encouraged him to feel it fully while focusing consciously on breathing.

Everything was designed to help him have his own connection with the true nature of his being, that place where God lives within us. Once there, I received a prompt, like a green light at a traffic stop. Once the *go* signal came, I guided him in the prayer:

"Marcus, God's showing me that anger needs to be addressed from a young age. Who was it that expressed anger most in your life?"

It didn't take long for him to point to the backyard. "My dad, for sure," he shared. "Growing up, he would be funny and witty one moment and blow up the next. I learned how to navigate his emotional state after stepping on a few too many *landmines*. At those times, the energy in the room would shift, and I dared not misstep. Dad's tone of voice would change, and he would often repeat himself. I learned to stop questioning in those moments and do whatever he asked. I became compliant."

"And what then?" I prompted him to continue.

"I would stay away and leave him alone while hiding out in my room or the basement. He couldn't lash out his anger at me if he couldn't find me. I could do whatever I wanted if I stayed away. But, if he did find me, he usually had something for me to do; mow the lawn, wash the dishes, clean, paint, or whatever else needed doing. I would do it angrily. I believed I didn't have a choice."

"But you did have a choice, didn't you?"

"I could have said 'no' to him, but never did."

"Why not," I pressed.

"Because he would spank me. That felt horrible, leading me to conclude that I was a bad person and I wanted to be good."

"Ok, we are right on it," I shared. "Let's continue. I am going to have you cancel some goals. Think of this as letting go of attachment to what you want, or wanted, that is mixed up in fear. For example, you were a good kid. Well, if you wanted to prove you were good after your dad spanked you, your reaction would be from fear, perhaps a fear that you were bad. Does that sound right?"

"Yes, right on," he said. "I wanted him to love me, to approve of me. I wanted to make things right."

"Exactly. Marcus, we want to collapse that charge of fear. Once you cancel the goal, you will feel any hidden emotions come up. If you are willing to feel them fully, your breath will move with the release of the emotions. If you find you are holding your breath, you are resisting the energy from releasing. You may fear what might come up with those feelings. It could be a disappointment that you were in that position, anger that your dad spanked you, or some other story. Whatever is buried with this issue can heal and change. These are like the 'demons' Jesus cast out. Releasing trapped energy from your system that is ready to leave will free you of its torment. Are you ready?"

"I think so. I'm ready." Marcus took a deep breath and closed his eyes, waiting for me to continue.

"Just repeat the following prompts out loud and pause until the energy that surfaces completes its cycle. It may intensify but will ultimately dissipate. Trust the process. This is how God taught me to heal dividedness in me. It was how Jesus taught people during his time. It is in the Bible for anyone with the eyes to see it. Here we go:

- "I cancel my goal to be a good boy.
- I release trying to change my situation.
- I accept my dad feeling angry and behaving how he behaved.
- I cancel my goal to heal my pain."

I had him pause, breathe, and be with his emotions between each statement. If he started out highly charged, a ten out of ten feelings, it might have come down to a six or seven but sometimes reduced to a zero or one. Making sure Marcus knew this was a process and not a one-time "fix," I told him that life consistently presents opportunities for us to address any unresolved parts until those wounds heal.

Marcus and I continued with many statements like those above, inviting the Holy Spirit to restore love where fear once ruled. We addressed hatred, hurt, fear, anxiousness, and all the rest rooted in the memories of dissociating from his life, abandoning his true nature in favor of fitting in, avoiding punishment, accepting flawed people as *perfect*, and making his home a sanctuary for hell in his mind.

I had an idea that Marcus stuffed away information, insights, potential opportunities, and life skills in favor of a victim mindset to punish his father. And, in doing so, he hurt himself the most. Other statements included:

- I release trying to change my past.
- I let go of hating people who are angry in my presence.
- I let go of hating people who took my choice away, real or imagined.
- I cancel my need to change how I feel and allow all my sensations to be felt (that was a big one).
- I accept my dad as he is and let go of who I perceived him to be.
- I let go of judging my parents.
- Love, God, come to me now and heal all that remains around this. God, guide me to wholeness with you.

And that was that. We finished with a simple but powerful prayer to invite God to guide him *home* to fully restore his life and be present as love.

Marcus looked happy. Supporting him in staying grounded, I told him that repairing the spirit may inspire him to seek what's needed to repair the rest of the parts (body, mind, emotions, etc.). "For example," I shared, "when I went through this, tests showed that my body severely lacked vitamin B and failed to process proteins properly, amongst other challenges." I wanted him to know lab work and skilled medical practitioners were critical to the body's well-being.

Note to reader: It is always recommended to see skilled practitioners. I prefer practitioners who believe in my capacity to heal fully. Consider alternatives if you work with someone who doesn't believe you can get well. Integrative and functional practitioners tend to look at the whole person and not just symptoms. There are doctors who believe healing from many mental illnesses is possible. I found them, and so can you.

I was about to get up when Marcus begged me, "please don't go. I feel so much better. I want more. Will you help me more?"

"Marcus, I certainly will, but try leaning into God first. You might find your healing path includes several resources. You prayed that I would show up when I was ready and here I am. Pray now for what is in your highest and best interests. It will become obvious if I am to be part of your ongoing healing process. But first, let what we just did integrate and open to what is best next."

Two weeks later, Marcus called me back to his home. We cleaned up the next piece that was ripe to address in his heart. And then, I asked him to try the following.

"Marcus, ask the Holy Spirit what you fear most right now. Once you ask, wait for an answer to come up through you. Let your brain relax. There is nothing to figure out here. Just wait and experience the voice of the Holy Spirit in you."

He asked and waited. As commonly happens when someone is learning, I received an inner prompt notifying me that he received an answer. I brought his attention to it by asking, "what was that?"

He paused and wasn't sure what to tell me. Then, as if rewinding the *tape* in his mind, he said, "I saw an image where I was hugging my dad, asking him to forgive me for holding on to child judgments for so long. I really saw me forgiving him."

"Great!" I exclaimed. "Now, go and hug him."

"Now?" He asked. "I don't know. He'll think that is weird. I haven't hugged him in thirty years."

"Marcus, The Holy Spirit gives us promptings. And we have free will to follow those prompts. If the insight is from love, you can trust it. But, if you are unsure, you can always ask, 'Holy Spirit, is it best to hug my dad right now?'"

He asked and nodded affirmatively. Looking outside, we could see his dad, Roger, once again in the yard. Marcus slowly stood and walked out to him. I remained in the kitchen and watched from the window over the sink. Marcus hugged his dad, who slowly lifted his arms and received the embrace. I could see both shaking from the emotions and staying in the hug as loved ones would after being apart for some time. When they finally let go, Marcus returned to the house as Roger watched him the entire way, wiping tears.

"How do you feel?" I asked when Marcus sat.

"Healed," he said. "I don't feel the pain I had before. My hatred. It's gone. How did you do that?"

"I didn't do anything, Marcus. Remember what happened. You asked for guidance from the Holy Spirit, and you received the prompting, and you trusted the prompting. You allowed God's love to heal you. That is how it works."

"Wow, I guess you're right. Thank you."

"You can do this anytime you want, Marcus. Get into a prayerful state, center yourself, connect with God's love, and ask for what is in your highest and best interests in that moment. Allow for God's love to inspire you. It always will. If you are agitated and fearful when you ask, then you will skew messages through that lens of fear or hostility. Those are not to be acted on as the outcomes will be negative and perhaps even harmful to yourself or others. Allow love to be your guide."

"But how will I know?" Marcus asked.

"You can tune into that loving state by imagining holding a newborn baby, puppy, or kitten. Imagine looking in their eyes and seeing the pure love from which they come. They are innocent, pure, perfect love. That will help you remember what love is. That is the state of being you want to be in when you pray for this guidance. Your path, if you choose it, is to maintain that loving space more and more in all areas of your life. The journey to that restoration will heal many past wounds and issues that repeat negatively in your life. It's a beautiful process."

"How do you know all this?" Marcus asked.

"Jesus taught all of us, and I am so thankful that he did."

"Wow. I love this. It's like the Holy Spirit is alive within me."

"Yes, Marcus, she is. Your body is the temple for the Holy Spirit, which lives within you. You are divinely attuning this temple to access Her immeasurable active forces consciously in your life."

"Divinely attuning?" Marcus asked.

"Yes. Jesus taught how to do this with the Beatitudes in concert with the Lord's Prayer. In fact, the first words of every Beatitude are 'blessed are', but that misses the depth of Jesus' meaning. He would have used a different word, 'touveyoun' in his Aramaic native tongue."

"Touveyhoun? I like the sound of that." Marcus said it aloud a few times before asking, "What does it mean?"

"It means latent within our human design is a GPS-like guidance system intended to be active and always guide us in alignment with divine will. When active, it leads to increased happiness and well-being. When not active, practicing the Beatitudes activates it!"

"Whoa!" Marcus exclaimed. "That sounds like tuning a radio antenna to God's frequency and receiving guidance right from the Source!!!!" Marcus was getting it.

"Yes, it won't take the action for you but will inform you perfectly. And the more you say yes or surrender to this Source guidance, the more aligned you are with God's Will. With your 'temple' divinely attuned, your relationship with the Holy Spirit grows. She unwinds the effects of your errors, corrects what is off, and brings you wisdom. She will teach you all things. It is quite spectacular.

"If you keep practicing them, the Beatitudes lead you to a

renewed relationship with God, one in being with the 'Father,' which is what Jesus prayed for in John 17: 20-23. He prayed for His followers to experience the same unity with God he experienced. Though you give up your life as you know it, you receive more in your new life. You'll know purpose, awe, love, freedom, courage, and true celebration. Fulfillment will be yours, something otherwise unattainable from this world. Keep practicing; God willing, you will transform and live as Marcus the Christ."

"I want this. I want it more than anything." Marcus shared.

"You have already started, and trust me, you are in good company. In the last Beatitude, Jesus tells us that all the prophets before us, those who awakened to Divine Purpose, have undergone this process.

"It is written in the Bible and on our hearts. It is available to all willing to go through their transformational experience. It can happen with grace and ease, or drama and trauma. Our choices matter. Our choices make a difference. Choosing love is the only choice that Christ chooses. Living as a Christ requires choosing love. As a result of this, I once again love my life, and believe you will too."

I wondered if I'd shared too much with Marcus. Just in case, I prayed for God to send him guidance, as well as to anyone else this message reaches, you included.

REFLECT & CONNECT
Chapters 16 & 17

Before moving forward, pause to reflect on your journey so far.

CH. 16: What does it mean to say "yes" to your purpose? The flowers remind Jack to fully embrace his purpose by saying "yes." What does saying "yes" to your own purpose look like? Are there areas of your life where fears and self-doubt hold you back from fully committing?

CH. 17: Role of forgiveness in healing: In this chapter, Marcus finds healing through forgiveness, particularly of his father. How does holding onto anger and resentment affect your emotional and spiritual well-being? What steps can you take to begin the process of forgiveness, either for yourself or others?

DIVE DEEPER - Join the conversation. Explore more thought-provoking questions and share your insights inside the **O Coalition Portal**.

Scan the QR Code to Enter the Discussion

thelowlyprophet.com/ tlp-reflect&connect

NEXT STEP
Walk the path. Live the transformation.

Hear **Jesus' native tongue of Aramaic** and experience the power of its resonance as you continue your Transformational Journey.

Scan to Explore the Aramaic Beatitudes & Lord's Prayer

thelowlyprophet.com/tlp-nextstep

ARAMAIC RESOURCES:

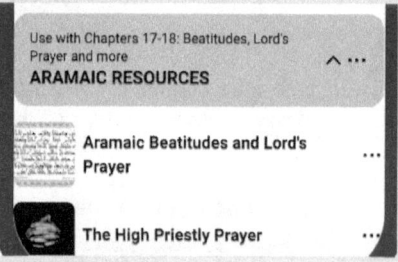

1. Locate **ARAMAIC RESOURCES** in the Syllabus

2. Watch, Listen, Read, and Practice.

Objective (Aramaic): Feel the power of the Beatitudes and Lord's Prayer spoken in Jesus' native tongue, Aramaic. Aramaic is a tonal language. Hearing and speaking the Beatitudes and Lord's Prayer has a transformative effect.

Objective (High Priestly Prayer): Tune in to the longest recorded prayer of Jesus Christ prays for their wholeness, union, to be as Jesus is with God follow by an explanation for deeper understanding.

CHAPTER 18
INTEGRATION

The next day at my kitchen table, I revisited the work with Marcus. At one point I asked Jesus for some insight. I was met with silence. Despite perceiving God would never abandon anyone, I still felt uncomfortable in the silence. "Jesus, what do I do? Where are you?" No answer came.

He wouldn't abandon me. I know it. Where did you go? Why aren't you answering? My stress intensified and Laura noticed.

"Jack, are you ok?" She interrupted my turmoil.

"Yeah, sure. Why?" I asked, looking up as she gathered food for lunch.

"You look troubled. Did something happen?"

I wasn't sure if I should tell her. Since my diagnosis I hadn't exactly advertised I regularly spoke with Jesus, and he spoke back. Even with her Jesus experience in high school, I still feared Laura perceiving me as crazy. After all, Jesus was a big theme in my hospitalizations, and I didn't want her to worry.

I know I'm not crazy now, but that doesn't mean others will agree. I need to trust Laura.

"Laura, I have a confession to make."

"Ok, I'm listening." She sat beside me and leaned in, touching my arm. Despite her compassionate eyes, memories of that look shifting to judgment surfaced. Past experiences told me if she felt scared, she would attack.

How do I approach this?

While consciously breathing, I started, "Listen. You know I am a bit weird. I mean, with all the crazy stuff we've been through, you know I've done things rather uniquely. Well, I've been talking to Jesus, and he talks back even when I'm sane. It's not just the few times you know about. It's quite often." I watched her eyes, expecting to see her question my sanity, but her expression didn't change. Perhaps recalling Jesus' high school visit helped her accept this part of me. I pressed forward.

"Laura, my beliefs have changed over the years. It may sound strange, but I am seeing God in everything, or just about everything. Jesus has taught so much about love, healing, and living. Divine insights have become so normal as I practice and integrate the Beatitudes more and more. It's remarkable. I don't always listen or interpret these divine messages correctly, but I'm getting better, and hindsight is proving the insights reliable and trustworthy."

"This sounds more like a testimony than confession, Jack. I

know all this. I've seen it. You don't have to hide anything from me."

Feeling emotional from her acceptance, as I thought I'd never receive it, I took a breath and continued, "Recent messages prompted me to visit Marcus this week, a guy I met in the hospital."

I shared the story with Laura. She was amazed that I saw a house, was given an address that turned out to be Marcus's home, and all the rest. She found it fascinating and questioned why I was troubled.

"Well," I answered, "I can't hear Jesus anymore. I've been trying, but he appears to have stopped talking to me."

"Jack, there must be a reason. Maybe there is a message in the silence. What feelings come about this?" She sounded supportive.

"Aloneness, isolation, feelings of emptiness. Like there is a void of content that once was accessible to me, and it's empty. "

"Do you have a goal running about this?" Laura knew the tools, and I appreciated her guiding me when my stress was up.

"I want him to keep talking with me so that I can feel good about myself."

"Are you willing to cancel that goal?"

"Laura, it is the one thing I have counted on to help me stay sane. Now I feel lost and afraid."

"It sounds like you're also running a goal to stay sane."

"You're damn right I am. I fear letting you down. I fear failing God or anyone else. I am afraid of failure." There it was. I could see the hidden fears now dancing at the surface of my mind.

"So, you have a goal to be successful and another to stay sane, and Jesus talking to you feels safe. Is that right?"

"Yes. Yes, that's right."

"Are you willing to cancel all your goals now?"

I felt calmer after that burst of anger passed through. "Yes, I am willing. I cancel my goals to stay sane." My breath moved involuntarily, and energy rushed up through my head. Pressure built in my right ear and then released. A wave of sadness came next, with a memory of disappointing my dad.

One summer night, I had hurt the kid next door and ran home to hide in my room. My dad found me. I told him what happened, and he was so disappointed I'd left the injured boy. He said we needed to see if my friend was okay. We walked a slow, silent, death march across the road to our neighbor's backyard where they celebrated a birthday with friends and family.

By the time we reached the boy's parents sitting in a circle of lawn chairs, I looked like a zombie. My dad asked about the boy's condition. Thankfully, he would be ok. Despite verbally accepting my apology, I noticed judgment in his mother's eyes. Instead of feeling compassion for the boy, I focused on my feelings of bitterness for getting caught and self-hate that I'd hurt a friend. That walk of shame haunted me for years, on guard against hurting anyone else and fearing, deep in my psyche, that I might be some sort of monster.

Recognizing all this as I sat with Laura, I cancelled more goals, "I cancel hiding my feelings. I allow this pain to surface. I release my judgments about Dad, my neighbors, and everyone who watched the spectacle unfold. I release judging and hating me for hurting my friend. I allow the truth. Holy Spirit, heal my denial and capacity to ever hurt anyone again. Heal my capacity to judge, self-punish or hate. I invite God's love to heal this, and anything associated with it. Restore me to my original state, love."

"There you go," Laura said. "You've got this. Keep going." She got up to finish preparing lunch while staying tuned-in to my progress.

"I release making up a story about what happened. I ask forgiveness for any sin of omission and sins of aggression. I release trying to get God to change my past. I allow myself to feel all emotions associated with this situation." My emotions arose with the power of a surfable wave, before crashing to *shore* as if the last of it was gone.

At that moment, I asked Jesus if there was anything else, and he responded. "No. You did it. I will always give you what you need most, Jack. In that moment, you needed silence to feel your emotions and access this hidden pain. This incident plagued your life since you were six. Great work. Way to stick with it!"

"Thank you, Jesus," I said out loud.

"Is he back?" Laura asked.

"Yeah. He never left. He just went silent for a moment. That was awesome. I love you, Laura. Thank you so much for your support."

"Of course. Now, let's eat."

And that was it. Laura didn't judge me at all. In fact, our relationship jumped to a whole new level. As it turned out, since her memory returned, she had been talking with Jesus too. She doesn't hear him like I do, but she knows he's there. She senses that he is with her and trusts that. That kind of faith is admirable.

After lunch, I tended to the garden while Laura left to share our abundance of vegetables with neighbors. The sun's rays pierced the clouds, landing on my shoulder along with an exquisite red and white butterfly. I looked up and noticed Jesus watching nearby.

His strong face and light-filled eyes always opened me further to God, melting away resistance and reminding me of God's powerful Life Force within me. Love poured forth in His presence.

"Jack, it's time," Jesus's words hit a nerve. The muscles in my neck tightened as my brain, trained to be still, stirred. Jesus continued. "Like that butterfly, your wings are strong.

It's time to take flight, Jack. Your message is needed now."

I trusted he was right, but still hoped this moment would be different. I'd imagined a fantasy graduation of sorts, with angels lifting me off to the heavens and putting this earthly life to rest.

He continued talking as I put down the shovel to embrace him. "This is the promise you made to yourself, Jack. You made it to me. You are one with the Creator of all things. Your voice: It's needed. Many will find their way through your words. Go, and extend God's grand invitation. People are waiting. They are ready."

Jesus looked on as a parent might when recognizing their child had grown into the unique, gifted, and amazing person anticipated. "Jack, you've seen many miracles, witnessed God, the great Abwoon in its glory, and reveled in the extraordinary. Remember the time you brought this caterpillar back to life?" He pointed to the red and white butterfly still fluttering through the garden.

"No, I don't," I squinted.

"Sure, you do. That caterpillar formed its chrysalis on a Milkweed you planted right there." He pointed to a collection of Milkweed to the side of the garden, surrounded by purple flowers and a bird bath mirroring the sky. "That tiny creature, Jack, gave up its life, only to be resurrected to its new life. Likewise, you have died and once again live. This is your resurrected life. You didn't dissolve your body, nor have nails pounded into your flesh, but you are no longer as you were, but live as you are, alive as a Christ in this world. You may recall the Apostle Paul described this when he said, "I have been crucified with Christ; yet I live, no longer I, but Christ lives in me" (Galatians 2:20 NABRE). Jack, stay in union, connected as one with God and your gifts will grow along with your impact. Let doubt and fear subside. Live in faith. You are worthy and enough. This isn't the end, Jack, but a milestone on an infinite adventure. Trust, you have what you need. Come now, let's reflect on your journey."

Jesus stretched his arms over my shoulders, cupping my head with intention. I felt my dusty brown hair fill in between his fingers as he brought our foreheads together to a gentle touch.

"Close your eyes, Jack. Think about when you and I met in the garden. Now, we begin."

Tears fell as I recalled my nephew's birthday party. What a glorious feeling. What a glorious day!!!

The End.

REFLECT & CONNECT
Chapters 18

Before moving forward, pause to reflect on your journey so far.

CH. 18: What does it mean to "take flight" in your life purpose? Jesus encourages Jack to embrace his calling and share his message with the world, symbolized by the butterfly taking flight. What does "taking flight" mean for you in your life purpose?

DIVE DEEPER - Join the conversation. Explore more thought-provoking questions and share your insights inside the **O Coalition Portal**.

Scan the QR Code to Enter the Discussion

thelowlyprophet.com/ tlp-reflect&connect

LIKE THIS BOOK?
YOUR REVIEW MATTERS.

If you enjoyed reading The Lowly Prophet and found its message meaningful, I would be incredibly grateful if you could leave an honest review on Amazon.

Reviews are vital for authors and help guide potential readers. Even sharing a few words about your favorite part or how the book impacted you can make a big difference. Your support is deeply appreciated.

thelowlyprophet.com/review-on-amazon

AFTERWORD

You are designed for success by the best designer ever, the God that created all. If you ask you shall receive. Knock and the door shall be opened. If you are interested in finding God all you need to do is seek. That said, many have come before us and opened doors, built bridges and created access where resistance once lived.

Below are some of the best resources on the planet to live as Christ. There are many more, but why not start where Jesus taught us to start?

Continue your adventure: Integrate the lessons Jack learned for yourself, heal your soul, and awaken the Christ in you. Three ways to start:

BEATITUDES PRACTICE

Connect with fresh eyes to the Sermon on the Mount as you discover the Beatitudes as a practice.

https://thelowlyprophet.com/tlp-beatitudespractice

COMMUNITY

Learn, practice, create, and connect with others committed to living as Christ.

https://thelowlyprophet.com/community

MENTAL HEALTH

Expand your knowledge of innovations in mental health through Journey's Dream's exceptional podcast (On Your Mind with Dr. Timothy J Hayes, PsyD), mentoring, and programs.

https://journeysdream.org/podcast

Like Jack experienced in our story, The Lowly Prophet came as a divine gift; a download from the Heavens. Read the origin story here:

ORIGIN STORY OF THE LOWLY PROPHET

August 24, 2023, I sat at my office table, meditating and praying about healing mental illnesses and undoing the root cause(s).

A familiar prompt from God's Holy Spirit came forth.

Continue reading story...
https://thelowlyprophet.com/originstory

IN CLOSING

No matter where you are or what you have done (or failed to do), God will find you if you ask. You will be happy you asked. Ask.

ACKNOWLEDGMENTS

To **God**, Who gave me this story to share. I love my life and so appreciate this wonderful opportunity to create and celebrate it!

To **Jesus**, Who showed us the way and unlocked a restorative path to Christ and holy re-union with God.

To **my family**, who I love with all my heart. May we find a home in Christ and live fully...all of us!

To **Melissa G. Wilson**, who believed in me when I felt alone in this project. Thank you for your wisdom, guidance, and encouragement throughout this journey.

To **Loren Michaels Harris**, who trusts in his divine promptings like few I have met. Loren invited me to join him at the opening of an event center in Naperville. That night he introduced me to Pia Renee.

To **Pia Renee**, who helped me get clear on what a prophet was the morning I began writing this book.

To **SubStack**, for providing an avenue to communicate easily and freely with a small community of friends and supporters early in the book process.

To **Colin Dingelstad,** who helped me launch @thelowlyprophet on Instagram and YouTube.

To **Karen Burton** for doing a wonderful developmental edit, bringing my raw writing to its polished state.

To **Milabookcovers.com** for an exceptional cover design!

To **Minista Jazz**, who delightfully created the beautiful chapter art.

To **Damian Jackson**, who created an excellent layout for the book and final edit.

To all **pre-release readers**, many of whom went above and

beyond with their time, talents, and input, this is a better book and better reading experience because of you.

To **CEO Space International**, Domingo Silvas, Jorge Raziel, Michael Cuatlal, Rofi Muhammad and all supporting the strategy, plan, tech, and marketing for The 'O' Coalition and The Lowly Prophet

To **Joseph Gabriel**, who, after being a pre-release reader, joined the team and has been incredibly helpful in supporting the book, technology, program and community launches.

To **Charlie Hattas**, who stepped in to transition The Lowly Prophet Transformation Journey (program) from one tech platform to another at a critical juncture.

To **Lynn Miller** who provided valuable insights for the book series and thorough review of materials with detailed support.

To **Illuminix Entertainment** and their brilliant team in helping share this wonderful message via The 'O' Coalition podcast, and for crafting an incredible logo and brand framework to support it. Thank you to Aaron, Jody, Lucinda and all behind the scenes.

To **Thought Leader Press** and Stefan Junaeus for partnering and collaborating to publish, promote, and share this work with a lot of people.

To all the significant influences on my faith and understanding of God, Jesus, and more, including the Bible, the Catholic Church (and schools); Dave and Susan Hattas (mom and dad); Dr. Michael J. Ryce (whyagain.org); Jayem (The Way of Mastery); Rex Montague-Bauer; Dennis Adams; Dale Allen Hoffman; Dr. Timothy J. Hayes; St. Teresa of Avila; St. Philomena; St. Thérèse, the Little Flower; Paulo Coelho (*The Alchemist*); Gary Renard (*The Disappearance of the Universe*); *A Course in Miracles*; The O Coalition; Jesus; and the Holy Spirit —all whose teachings influenced me and the characters in this novel.

ABOUT THE AUTHOR

God has given Mark Hattas a gift to support people healing divisions within themselves and live fully as the expressions of love God has created each of us to be.

He does this through writing, speaking, and coaching.

The Lowly Prophet is the first in a series to guide readers through spiritual healing, development, and restoration.

Follow on Instagram: instagram.com/thelowlyprophet
Follow on YouTube: youtube.com/@thelowlyprophet
Stay connected: thelowlyprophet.com

Mark is a certified mental performance coach, spiritual healing coach, seven-time author, and entrepreneur. He was honored with a Ph.D. in Entrepreneurship & Business (h.c.) from TIUA School of Business, recognizing his achievements in executive and mental performance coaching, entrepreneurship, business, and charitable contributions to mental health.

Learn more at: thelowlyprophet.com/mark

ENDNOTES

- Yonan Codex Foundation, *Enlightenment: Selected Passages From The Aramaic New Testament, HeartLand 2014 Edition.* HeartLand Publications, 2014.
- Hattas, Mark, Dave Austin, and Cathy Lynn. *The BeAttitudes Practice.* beatitudespractice.com, 2024. Accessed July 27, 2024. https://beatitudespractice.com.
- Ryce, Michael, Dale Allen Hoffman, and Mark Hattas. "The Be-Attitudes From the Aramaic." *Why Is This Happening to Me... AGAIN?!*, whyagain.org, 2024. Accessed July 27, 2024. https://whyagain.org/khabouris-be-attitudes/.
- Jayem. "Aramaic Beatitudes." *One Who Wakes*, 2013. Accessed July 27, 2024. https://www.onewhowakes.org/wp-content/uploads/2013/07/WOM-Aramaic-Beatitudes1.pdf?x21307.
- Teachings and methods utilized by the characters in this novel are inspired by the works of Jesus and the Holy Spirit. Original material can be found in the

Bible and through your invitation of the Holy Spirit to guide your life.

- Some teachings and methods utilized by the characters in this novel are inspired by the works of Dr. Michael J. Ryce. For more information on his material, please refer to Dr. Ryce's publications and resources available at whyagain.org. While this novel incorporates tools and concepts developed by Michael Ryce, the specific applications and narrative presented are fictional and created for the purposes of this story.
- Any resemblance to real persons, living or dead, or actual events is purely coincidental.